MW01291656

Ghost Writings

Ghost Writings
A Ghost Story Guide

Edited by
Deborah Bennison

Introductory notes by
Neil Wilson

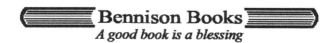
Bennison Books
A good book is a blessing

Introductory notes by Neil Wilson, author of
Shadows in the Attic
A Guide to British Supernatural Fiction 1820-1950
(British Library, 2000)

With special thanks to Daisy Bennison

Cover by idrewdesign and fayefaye designs

A Bennison Books People's Classic
ISBN 978-1-499-29488-0

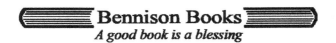

Bennison Books
A good book is a blessing

Contents

Foreword

Welcome to this ghost story guide, written with the generous assistance of Neil Wilson, author of the definitive British ghost story bibliography, *Shadows in the Attic* (British Library, 2000).

The ghost story genre is quieter than its bigger, brasher science fiction and horror relations. It sits patiently in a corner or behind closed doors, never quite leaving and always waiting to be rediscovered. Perhaps too often underestimated and dismissed as lightweight entertainment, it is notable that a number of leading literary figures took the genre seriously and were keen to grapple with and master the form; they recognised the challenges it posed and how fiendishly difficult it is to write successful ghostly fiction. Newcomers to the genre may be pleasantly surprised by the skill, subtlety and psychological insight displayed by the master ghost story writers. The finest examples transcend the genre and take their place among the best of our classic literature.

Notes

This volume is an introduction to the ghost story genre compiled with the aim of inspiring the reader to explore further. It concentrates particularly on the rich heritage of British ghost fiction, and for this reason American authors in the genre are not included in the author biographies. It should also be noted that the selected bibliographies included with author details are not comprehensive and often include publications that are now out of print; they are mentioned solely for historical interest. However, many of these works are now widely available in new print and electronic editions and can be readily found on Amazon.

Some authors are included in more than one section in this volume. For example, those authors listed under 'masters of the genre' may also appear in the 'literary' section and/or the section on female writers in the genre.

DB

The Appeal of the Supernatural

Neil Wilson

That we should remain so fascinated by the supernatural in the most technologically advanced era in human history is arguably an example of the very irrationality Edgar Allen Poe once characterised as 'the imp of the perverse'.

After a period of profound scientific advance, it is paradoxical that the appeal of the supernatural remains irresistible and profound. Arguably, the Canute-like response of the occult revivals of the 1890s and 1960s to the rising tide of scientific explanation can be understood as answering a basic human need for the mysterious, wondrous and inexplicable.

The idea of the supernatural constantly evolves to reflect contemporary fashions and obsessions. The Victorian spiritualist movement gave way to New Age 'channelling'; sophisticated Renaissance astrology became popular entertainment; and Europe's vampire aristocrats have metamorphosed into superheroes or teen martial artists. Equally, the violence and horror of the modern world are reflected in increasingly gory supernatural encounters in fiction.

On rare occasions, science itself has been called upon to rationalise the supernatural, rather than debunk and dismiss it. Groups, including the Society for Psychical Research, scientists, such as Dr J.B. Rhine, and amateur ghost hunters, including the notorious Harry Price, have tried and failed to establish verifiable facts.

Fact and fiction

The evolution of popular ideas about the supernatural owes as much to fictional invention as it does to factual or scientific discoveries. The treatments of subjects such as vampirism and demonic possession developed an increasingly symbiotic relationship, with fiction sometimes accepted and presented as fact. An example of this is the creation of elements of vampire and werewolf mythology by script writers of 1930s Universal horror films, much of which is now cited as fact in non-fiction sources.

The supernatural has always resisted either verification or disproof and it continues to retain its enduring fascination and strong hold on the public imagination.

But what exactly is the supernatural?

Oxford Dictionaries (online) defines the supernatural as 'a manifestation or event attributed to some force beyond scientific understanding or the laws of nature'.

So in its broadest definition, the supernatural encompasses a huge range of topics. In addition to the conventional ghost story, these include fairy tales or folk legends, perhaps involving witches or talking animals; fictionalised accounts of 'true' hauntings; and metaphysical fantasies about miraculous events or battles against the forces of evil. In summary, anything contrary to or outside the laws or conventions of the natural world can be classified as supernatural.

4

The unnatural

The cornerstone of the supernatural fiction tradition is undoubtedly the concept of the 'unnatural'. Dictionary definitions of the supernatural allow the possibility of miraculous and positive intervention in human affairs by divine or superhuman forces. However, the popular idea of a supernatural tale commonly involves the malign activities of evil entities whose actions defy the accepted world order in some way. This basic message is usually underlined by a cumulative use of disturbing motifs or details which imply that the rules governing the predictable everyday world are beginning to break down.

Sometimes, as in Walter De La Mare's celebrated short story *All Hallows* (1926) supernatural powers attempt to create a sacrilegious parody of the normal world to further their evil intent. In others, the true horror of works such as Henry James' masterpiece *The Turn of the Screw* (1898) lies in the implied corruption of children as basic symbols of purity.

The ancient and the modern

Tales of malevolent supernatural forces can be traced back to the beginning of history and have been recorded by anthropologists investigating human cultures worldwide. The ubiquity of this material suggests its fundamental importance to us as an explanation for seemingly inexplicable events involving human misfortune.

While society's fortunes were believed to be dependent

5

on the gods, an individual's or family's fate could more easily be ascribed to the activities of lower level and more capricious or malign forces. A common feature of most supernatural tales throughout history is their relatively small scale; this eventually became perfect short story material, leading ultimately to the creation of the classic ghost story format.

In contrast, tales attempting to explain the fate of societies or nations necessarily required a broader canvas and often became the foundation of national myths. While some authors, such as Charles Williams, have attempted to create large-scale supernatural novels exploring metaphysical issues, such as *War in Heaven* (1930), few have been successful, the content often seeming closer to fictionalised theology than supernatural fiction.

However, it is notable that a decline in the acceptance of religious dogma during the twentieth century was accompanied by a rise in the popularity of science fiction. This development saw the age-old millenarian threat of invading demonic forces of the 'last days' replaced by modern cosmic myths of alien invasions.

The individual versus the unknown

The predominant form of the supernatural tale is essentially that of an individual's encounter with the unknown; the narrative is often in the first person to allow ambiguity in the interpretation of events. Commonly, the protagonist might be responsible, intentionally or not, for breaking some social or religious convention and inevitably suffers the consequences. This disruption of the natural order often allows evil supernatural forces to surface. However, in punishing the transgressor these supernatural forces restore and reinforce the status quo by healing a potential rift in the social order. Their work done, they usually swiftly return to their proper place beyond the normal everyday world.

In other cases, the individual might be the plaything of amoral but powerful supernatural forces, or the victim of an evil member of society, such as a witch or black magician, who transgresses by calling upon supernatural powers. Classical mythology contains numerous examples of individuals who become sport of the gods. While this specific motif has become less popular, the idea of an individual falling prey to ghostly or demonic forces lying in wait for the unwary remains a common one.

Influences from beyond the grave

In many ancient cultures, particularly strong beliefs were held about death and the correct treatment of corpses. Complex rituals were often enacted to prevent the dead from interfering with the activities of the living. The malevolent influence of those who died unnatural or violent deaths, such as suicide, murder or execution, was especially feared and forms the basis of many supernatural tales. Such legends often suggest that if something unnatural had occurred, redress would inevitably be required, even if this might take centuries to achieve. Given this versatile raw material, numerous variations were explored by later writers in the supernatural genre.

Necromancy, or the conjuration of the spirits of the dead, was long held in particular abhorrence despite its biblical origins with King Saul and the Witch of Endor. It is notable, however, that a resurgence of interest in the subject under the new guise of spiritualism during the nineteenth century coincided with the high point of Victorian religiosity.

A common belief at the beginning of the nineteenth century was that of the 'restless dead'. Often, these would be ghosts forced to walk because of unfinished business related to their violent deaths or the sins they committed while alive. The ghost might be a victim, a perpetrator of a crime, or someone unjustly accused needing the intervention of a living person to correct past wrongs and bring them peace.

However, equally prevalent and closer to the roots of the ghost tradition was a belief in malign individuals who attempt to perpetuate their evil lives beyond the grave. This provided some of the most fertile ground for the development of supernatural fiction.

The idea of the evil spirit overlaps with that of the demonic force whose mythology was elaborated considerably during the European witch hunts of the Middle Ages. The ideas explored in works such as Jean Bodin's *De la Démonomanie des Sorciers* (1580), Nicholas Remy's *Demonolatreiae* (1595) and Jakob Sprenger and Heinrich Kramer's infamous *Malleus Maleficarum* (1486) pervaded popular culture, providing more material for authors of supernatural fiction. For example, the concept of the witch's familiar, together with the related idea of the magician's demonic pact, inspired numerous early stories, from the Faust legend to Harrison Ainsworth's novel, *The Lancashire Witches* (1849).

Neil Wilson 2014

The Evolution of the Ghost Story

Neil Wilson

B ritish supernatural fiction is most commonly associated with the ghost story. Between 1820 and 1950, a period known today as the golden age of British ghost fiction, the traditional ghostly tale was adopted as a mainstream literary form by many of the foremost writers of the era. It came to dominate the supernatural genre, reaching a level of mastery that many believe remains unmatched to this day.

While the supernatural has long been a rich source of artistic inspiration, it is more recently over the past two centuries that its present status as a cornerstone of popular culture was firmly established. Many of the most popular and enduring themes and motifs of supernatural fiction appeared for the first time during this period. The genre evolved from the bizarre and increasingly formulaic world of Gothic fiction to encompass material as diverse as the pulp horror of the Victorian 'penny bloods'; the morality tales of bestselling authors, including Charles Dickens and Mrs Gaskell; and works of great psychological sophistication created by lesser-known writers such as Oliver Onions and Robert Hichens.

Historical background

The concept of the ghost can be found in most cultures and has been recorded in a wide range of historical sources from the legends of Ancient Greece to the Old

Testament. However, it was in Roman literature, that ghosts first became more than legendary background material and were depicted as interacting directly with human beings. Here we see the earliest foundations of the ghost tradition.

The horrific plagues and witch persecutions of the Middle Ages contributed to the development of numerous supernatural myths and legends. The 'dance of death' and personification of the 'grim reaper' remain powerful motifs from this period and their potency endures to the present day.

However, the fictional ghost story was rare, with supernatural encounters usually presented in the context of popular mystery plays or simply related as true events. The latter tradition would last well into the eighteenth century with accounts of Smithfield's notorious Cock Lane Ghost (1762) and Daniel Defoe's *True Relation of the Apparition of One Mrs Veal* (1706).

While ghostly apparitions did occasionally appear in drama, such as Shakespeare's *Hamlet* (1600) and *Macbeth* (1606), this was a relatively infrequent occurrence. They were often a throwback to older stage traditions revived to reflect a renewed interest in the supernatural, as happened, for example, during the reign of King James I of England, who wrote *Demonology* (1597). Ironically, the king's strong belief in the existence of witchcraft would eventually change to one of scepticism following his personal investigation into the subject.

It was not until the advent of the Gothic novel and the

birth of the Romantic movement during the late eighteenth century that ghosts became common literary figures, albeit in rather stylised and restricted forms. In ever more desperate attempts to exceed the sensationalism of the latest Gothic bestsellers, authors created increasingly melodramatic and implausible works that eventually turned Gothic staples, such as haunted castles, skeletal ghosts, clanking chains and ancestral curses, into tired clichés.

However, while parodies, most notably Jane Austen's *Northanger Abbey* (1818), lampooned the Gothic novel, the genre was important in creating popular interest in supernatural themes and laying the foundations for the later ghost story tradition. Gothic ghosts were regularly used to introduce colourful historical background material and this forged the traditional association of ghosts with events from the distant past. This idea would endure long after the popularity of the Gothic genre faded, with the antiquarian ghost stories of later writers, such as A.N.L. Munby, Frederick Cowles and M.R. James, using historical ghosts to create sophisticated and satisfying works of supernatural literature.

The golden age of the ghost story

The origins of the classic ghost story can be traced to the emergence of a more naturalistic style of writing during the early nineteenth century, partly in reaction to previous Gothic excess. While writers such as Sir Walter Scott in *The Monastery* (1820) and Harrison Ainsworth in *Rookwood* (1834) occasionally used Gothic effects or motifs, their work signalled the beginnings of a new era in which authors would move ghosts increasingly centre stage to write fiction of considerable psychological and motivational complexity.

The contemporary popularity of historical subjects for novels and short stories allowed for easy introduction of ghostly episodes into mainstream works for dramatic effect or light relief. An early example is Sir Walter Scott's inclusion of the self-contained ghost story *Wandering Willie's Tale* in his novel *Redgauntlet* (1824). However, the most famous example is probably the appearance of Cathy's ghost in Emily Brontë's *Wuthering Heights* (1847).

Classic features

It was the Irish author, Joseph Sheridan Le Fanu, who most successfully built on the foundations of the Gothic style, introducing a more realistic approach to create a new and popular type of supernatural fiction. In a series of ghost stories and mystery novels beginning with *The Ghost and the Bone Setter* (1838) and culminating with the seminal collection *In a Glass Darkly* (1872), Le Fanu developed many classic features of the Victorian ghost story tradition. The influence of these works on both his contemporaries and later writers, most notably M.R. James, was considerable, and helped define the style of mainstream ghost fiction for several generations.

The popularity of the ghost story grew considerably during the 1840s and 1850s, supplementing the increasingly wide choice of literature to which the reading public now had access. This varied from the sensationalist pulp horror of the 'penny bloods' and popular magazines, including Charles Dickens' *All the Year Round* and *Household Words*, to novels available from the new lending libraries. In the competitive world of commercial publishing, editors constantly sought to identify and satisfy any popular demand from their readers. The ghost story offered an appealing medium through which to address multiple Victorian obsessions, from morality and death to sublimated sex, in a form highly suited to magazine publication. Meanwhile, across the Atlantic, American authors such as Edgar Allan Poe and Nathaniel Hawthorne also saw the literary potential of the supernatural for exploring the darker frontiers of fiction.

New influences

In the final years of the nineteenth century, a number of new influences and preoccupations were reflected in supernatural literature. Spiritualism, which had influenced much ghostly fiction since the 1850s, was by this time just one of many occult movements. Organisations such as the Theosophical Society and magical societies like the Hermetic Order of the Golden Dawn offered a supernatural alternative to those increasingly disenchanted with the inexorable rise of materialism and scientific rationalism. Many writers were attracted to the Golden Dawn in particular; its membership list was a contemporary who's who of supernatural fiction.

At the same time, the decadent artistic movement

spawned an interest in all things exotic or bizarre, including the supernatural. The movement was characterised by a richly verbose purple prose style which influenced much genre writing of the period. While many writers, most notably M.R. James, continued to produce traditional ghostly tales, others, including Arthur Machen, M.P. Shiel and Robert Murray Gilchrist, experimented with wider influences, often incorporating occult references to create ever more fantastic forms of supernatural writing.

Complex and sophisticated

The evolution of more complex and sophisticated forms of the ghost story was matched by a growing stylistic maturity. The highly influential works of the Cambridge academic M.R. James, including *Ghost Stories of an Antiquary* (1904), represent a high point in the development of the genre and he is widely considered to have written near-perfect examples of the ghost story form.

James' ideas on ghost fiction (his essay on the subject is included in this volume) were derived from a detailed study of previous masters of the genre, most notably Sheridan Le Fanu, and throw considerable light on the essential components for successful supernatural writing.

Central, he asserts, is the development of a credible ghostly atmosphere, the subtle handling of which is crucial for the suspension of disbelief. Once suitable background details have been established and the scene set, supernatural elements may gradually be introduced, ideally in a manner that preserves some degree of ambiguity until a final swift and dreadful climax is achieved.

James' ground rules would be taken up and used by many later writers, although rarely as successfully as in James' own stories. While highly sophisticated in execution, it is interesting to note that James' works exploit some of the oldest themes of supernatural fiction and feature classic examples of ghosts as agents of retribution, redressing past or present wrongs.

Continuing popularity

The evolution in stylistic sophistication, psychological complexity and an increasingly varied range of background material and settings allowed the ghost story to remain popular, even during the more conventional horrors of the First World War. The form also proved flexible enough to be used for propaganda purposes during the conflict, for example, in the works of Frederick Britten Austin and Arthur Machen. Indeed, many believed Machen's *The Bowmen* (1914) was a factual account of angelic intervention on the Western Front and it led to the creation of the myth of the 'Angels of Mons' who were thought to have protected the British army during the Battle of Mons.

The demand for escapist literature continued throughout the inter-war period with ghost story collections by traditional authors such as M.R. James and Algernon Blackwood being complemented by those of a younger generation of popular writers, including H.R. Wakefield and Hugh Walpole. Ghost story anthologies, such as Montague Summers' *The Supernatural Omnibus* (1931) and Dennis Wheatley's *A Century of Horror Stories* (1935), introduced a new generation to many classics of the genre.

Charles Birkin's *Creeps* series and Lady Cynthia Asquith's *Ghost Books* helped maintain the demand for new material. Birkin and Asquith commissioned tales from mainstream literary figures such as L.P. Hartley and D.H. Lawrence as well as popular genre writers, including Elliot O'Donnell and Algernon Blackwood.

Blackwood was also instrumental in introducing a new radio-listening audience to the genre. As the once prolific writer's output gradually diminished, he developed a new career as a BBC broadcaster. But although the traditional ghost story worked reasonably well on radio, it was to prove rather less successful in film and on television.

Sensationalism

The introduction of illustrations into the popular magazines of the late Victorian era had already begun to change the nature of ghost fiction by requiring shorter stories with swifter plot development. While this suited the faster pace of adventure and crime fiction, it was less satisfactory for the traditional ghost story, forcing cruder atmospheric development and demanding graphic horrors for illustrators to portray.

This situation was compounded in the cinema where audiences expected fast-moving plots and ever more sensational special effects. This growing appetite for sensationalism had little time for the subtleties of traditional ghost fiction.

Following the death of M.R. James in 1936, his publisher Edward Arnold attempted to find new talent to replace their bestselling ghost story author. However, the world had moved on and while some new writers were hopefully put forward to take James' place, it seemed that the days of the classic ghost story were numbered. The genre now appeared increasingly anachronistic in a world where technology and science encouraged the public to look forward, rather than back.

The post-war period

The real-life horrors of the Second World War did little to diminish the public demand for terrifying fiction. However, pictures of the skeletal figures of Belsen and the charred silhouettes of Hiroshima meant imaginary horrors would need to be taken to new levels to create the catharsis sought by post-Holocaust audiences.

As a result, a darker more pessimistic tone crept into post-war supernatural fiction, with graphic depictions of physical horror often supplanting those of supernatural phenomena. Perhaps more disturbing was the disappearance from many supernatural tales of a basic moral context.

The malevolent ghosts in earlier works usually appeared to correct some ancient wrongdoing and harm was rarely visited on the just; a traditional ghost story might be unsettling but it also reinforced the belief that a strong, if occasionally fearsome, moral order existed. However, the supernatural forces of post-war fiction often had greater similarities with the muggers of a modern city, preying on any vulnerable individual they chanced to encounter with terrifying ferocity.

Amoral cosmic horror

This trend had already begun in the work of pre-war American writers, most notably H.P. Lovecraft, who had themselves been influenced by earlier British authors such as Arthur Machen and William Hope Hodgson.

Lovecraft's amoral brand of cosmic horror attempted to blend science and the supernatural on the largest of scales. His preoccupation with the blind indifference of the universe to an individual's fate fitted perfectly with the more existential world view of the post-war era.

One of Lovecraft's admirers was the writer Robert Bloch. Originally inspired by Lovecraft's style, he went on to create one of the most influential works of modern horror fiction, *Psycho* (1959). Bloch heralded an era in which authors increasingly wrote with one eye firmly fixed on a potentially lucrative film adaptation.

Film and large-scale novels

In Britain, writers such as Dennis Wheatley, and later, James Herbert and Clive Barker, blended elements of the British and American supernatural traditions with aspects of thriller and horror fiction to develop fast-moving horror-based works. This approach was more suitable for both film and the large-scale novels which had by now taken over from the short story as the most popular medium for supernatural fiction.

It is essential for the vitality of any genre to retain its relevance by continually evolving to reflect aspects of the world in which its readers live. However, the increasingly visual nature of popular media, coupled with a need to continually stretch boundaries in the search for originality and ever more sensational effects, has a number of potential limitations. Taken to extremes, the disturbing effect of gross depictions of physical horror combined with an amoral or overly pessimistic approach can simply drain and depress readers.

In addition, the need to constantly exceed previous levels of sensationalism becomes increasingly problematic as we are desensitised and the material we are presented with begins to approach self-parody in a way reminiscent of the final days of the Gothic era.

A revival

After a period of some neglect, a renewed interest in more traditional supernatural stories began in the 1960s during the occult revival which formed part of the contemporary search for alternative lifestyles.

Interest in the more fantastical fiction of authors such as Arthur Machen and William Hope Hodgson was followed by a revival of the work of more mainstream figures, including Algernon Blackwood and Vernon Lee. Many stories appeared in paperback for the first time, with numerous supernatural fiction anthologies, most notably Fontana's *Great Ghost Stories* series, achieving significant sales and inspiring many readers to explore the genre further.

Tireless anthologists and bibliographers, including Peter Haining, Hugh Lamb and Richard Dalby, located and collected numerous rare items from both classic and more obscure authors. The result of their painstaking work is a more complete picture of supernatural fiction during the past two centuries than was previously possible. Their dedicated work continues with the regular discovery of material by a new generation of writers and scholars, including Mike Ashley, Jack Adrian and Jessica Amanda Salmonson.

A particularly valuable development has been a greater appreciation and acknowledgement of the contribution made by female writers to the genre, many of whom have long resided in ill-deserved obscurity until their revival in collections by publishers such as Virago.

Academic study

Supernatural fiction has also been subject to an increasing degree of academic study, with writers such as Michael Cox, Jack Sullivan and Julia Briggs making important contributions to the critical literature of the genre.

Due to the limited quantity of high quality original material, some authors, backed by an increasingly sophisticated group of small publishers, have attempted to write new stories in the style of past masters such as M.R. James.

Rosemary Pardoe's imprint, Haunted Library, was responsible for the publication of much new material in the antiquarian tradition by writers such as Ron Weighell and David Rowlands, as well as several previously unknown items by James in the periodical *Ghosts and Scholars*.

Writers, including Ramsay Campbell, have also taken inspiration from authors such as James and have updated the traditional ghost story with a contemporary twist.

Enduring appeal

The huge success of Peter Straub's novel *Ghost Story* (1979) proved it was still possible to create large-scale supernatural novels of subtle complexity. One can see in such works a measured retreat from the grosser aspects of modern supernatural horror.

The revival of interest in the traditional ghost story continued with Susan Hill's *The Woman in Black* (1983), the first significant novel in the genre by a mainstream British author for over 50 years, also successfully adapted for stage and screen.

The enduring appeal of the supernatural may be due to its very intangibility. In addition, its ability to metamorphose enables it to reflect contemporary concerns and preoccupations while providing the perfect platform to explore eternal human questions of death, morality, redemption, retribution and human frailty.

Paradoxically, the brighter the light of scientific reason burns, the darker and more elusive are the shadows that remain.

Neil Wilson 2014

Common Supernatural Themes and Topics

Neil Wilson

The curse and revenge

A common motif in the supernatural fiction tradition is the idea of the curse which is used to explore the basic concepts of transgression and revenge. The emphasis is on the ability of the poor and powerless to call on supernatural retribution and redress for evil acts committed by the rich and powerful. The curse cannot be lifted until the wrong is corrected, either by the perpetrator or their successors, further underlining the timeless nature of the moral forces involved.

The curse has proven to be an enduringly popular and versatile theme, resonating well with Gothic and Romantic narratives about individuals fighting ill-fated destinies. In many instances, the concept of fate also allowed authors to draw on traditions concerning premonition or second sight to use as background material.

Many variations emerged over time, from the curse of the werewolf to the ancient Irish tradition of the banshee, a spirit who would inform a cursed family of the impending death of a member of their clan.

In addition, the vengeful ghosts of some traditions are materialistic spirits who covet the physical pleasures of the world and try to feed off the energies of vulnerable individuals to sustain a tenuous link with life. One can trace the origins of both the European vampire tale and the more ancient concept of spirit possession to such ideas. Similarly, the German poltergeist or 'noisy ghost' might attempt to possess a building, often their former home, because they cannot accept death and resent the 'intruders' who have taken their place.

Folklore

Depictions of the 'Gentry' or fairy folk have metamorphosed considerably over time. Numerous folk tales describe the dangers of angering the 'little people' or related nature spirits and suggest how to appease them and preserve good fortune. Others warn of the possibility of fairy changeling children being swapped for one's own, or tell of the fate of those kidnapped for interrupting fairy rituals in lonely spots.

Despite the evolution of the saccharine Victorian children's fairy tale, authors such as Sheridan Le Fanu and Arthur Machen, who lived in regions where fairy beliefs had not entirely died out, were inspired by stories of potentially malevolent Irish and Welsh fairies to create some of their most original and powerful work.

Folklore was the foundation of many of the earliest stories in the supernatural genre and some authors' re-working of this material clearly demonstrates its folk origins. Writers such as Catherine Crowe in *The Night Side of Nature* (1848) presented fictionalised accounts of supposedly true hauntings in what might today be described as faction. Other authors, such as James Hogg in *The Shepherd's Calendar* (1829), rework old legends in a modern style to attract a wider readership; the often bizarre and unreal nature of such stories causes some works to stray into fantasy. Authors such as Lord Dunsany created new mythologies in this genre borderland which proved highly influential on later generations of writers.

Crossover works

While the Gothic and supernatural fiction genres share common roots and often similar subjects, they are not the same. Daphne Du Maurier's masterpiece *Rebecca* (1938) has an identifiably Gothic flavour without being in the least supernatural, while in Emily Brontë's *Wuthering Heights* (1847), the supernatural content is incidental to the main plot. The conventions of Gothic or supernatural fiction have also been used to build an atmosphere of menace while omitting supernatural content. Sometimes, non-supernatural works simply refer to ghostly events of the past for background colour.

However, a considerable number of stories could be classified as supernatural works with Gothic features or vice versa, depending on the predisposition of the reader.

Some works, such as Horace Horsnell's *Castle Cottage* (1940), use elements common to Romantic novels, while others, including Robert Marshall's *The Haunted Major* (1902) and Oscar Wilde's *The Canterville Ghost* (1891), are also classics of humorous fiction.

In addition, the simple desire to create popular and commercially rewarding entertainment might be seen as a reason why writers such as Dennis Wheatley and Sax Rohmer introduced features from thriller and adventure fiction into their work. For others, the motivation is more complex.

Science fiction and the supernatural

While some crossover has taken place between the science fiction and supernatural genres, this has been one of the least fertile areas of development. The fundamental difference between scientific rationalism and supernatural irrationalism proves an insurmountable obstacle for most authors. Occasionally, however, writers such as David Lindsay in *A Voyage to Arcturus* (1920) and Arthur Machen in *The Great God Pan* (1894) have managed to create successful hybrid works that call on features from both genres.

Often, ghosts or other supernatural phenomena are featured but later explained away as fakery, dreams or illusions. The author Eden Phillpotts, for example, includes seemingly ghostly events in his works – usually as a cover for criminal activities – only to later debunk them. Variations of this plot type have proved enduringly popular in films such as *The Cat and the Canary* (1939) and even children's television series like *Scooby Doo*.

The occult detective

One of the most popular supernatural crossover areas

is undoubtedly crime fiction. The gradual discovery of clues in an attempt to explain supernatural events has much in common with detective fiction.

An entire 'occult detective' sub-genre has grown up in this area, with some of supernatural fiction's most popular writers creating series detectives such as William Hope Hodgson's Carnacki, Algernon Blackwood's John Silence and Dion Fortune's Dr Taverner.

The rise in popularity of detective fiction, most notably Arthur Conan Doyle's Sherlock Holmes series, coupled with the contemporary occult revival inspired several authors to combine ghost and crime story formats in what became a new occult detective sub-genre. While the roots of this material may be traced back to early works such as Sir Edward Bulwer Lytton's *The Haunted and the Haunters* (1860), it reached the height of its popularity during the first two decades of the twentieth century. However, although the occult detective style enabled the expansion of the traditional ghost story format, all too often authors over-used pseudo-occultist jargon in unsuccessful attempts to convey authenticity.

 Even key exponents of the occult detective sub-genre, such as Algernon Blackwood and William Hope Hodgson, were not without fault and many works now seem dated and unsatisfactory. Although the occult detective format has been revisited by authors over the years, it has proven to be one of the most difficult to successfully realise. One of the better examples is E and H Heron's 'Flaxman Low' series of stories, collected in *Ghosts* (1899), which were admired by both Arthur Conan Doyle and M.R. James.

The evolving relationship between science fiction, horror, crime fiction and the supernatural has ultimately led to a blurring of boundaries in the popular imagination. Tales such as Robert Louis Stevenson's *The Strange Case of Dr Jekyll and Mr Hyde* (1886) blend elements from each to create modern morality tales with science enabling miraculous transformations that would previously have been attributed to the supernatural.

Religion and the occult

Many authors have used the supernatural genre to explore their own beliefs. These range from Algernon Blackwood's tales of nature mysticism in *The Lost Valley and Other Stories* (1910) to spiritualist novels, including Marie Corelli's *A Romance of Two Worlds* (1886), and occultist fantasies such as Dion Fortune's *The Demon Lover* (1927). The stories of religious writers, including Roger Pater in *Mystic Voices* (1923) and R.H. Benson in *The Light Invisible* (1903), are permeated by their personal faith and desire to convey Catholic doctrine to others.

However, an author's belief in the authenticity of their subject matter often proves an obstacle to the creation of successful supernatural fiction. Commonly, the use of arcane occult jargon disrupts the flow of plots instead of contributing additional validity. In contrast, it is testimony to the skill of some of the genre's most effective writers, such as Oliver Onions, that their scepticism of the supernatural did not prevent them creating some of its best tales.

Something old, something new

Writers of supernatural fiction have always been willing to integrate new and fashionable motifs into their work or modernise tried and tested themes to attract an increasingly sophisticated and sensation-hungry public. Examples can be found throughout the nineteenth and twentieth centuries as archaeological and anthropological discoveries were made and widely publicised.

Authors whose raw material had previously been limited to the folk traditions of their native regions could now draw on a wide range of sources, from exotic supernatural creations, such as Haitian zombies or African witch doctors, to subjects from the distant past, such as Ancient Egyptian magic. The latter proved to be an exceptionally popular source of inspiration, with countless stories, including Bram Stoker's *The Jewel of Seven Stars* (1903), exploring themes such as the curse of the pharaohs, vengeful mummies and reincarnation.

Other writers simply updated the traditional trappings of the supernatural for an increasingly industrialised age, leaving the original plots largely intact. The phantom coach of previous generations became a motor car in William Fairlie Clarke's *The Mystery of Chickerly Grange* written during the 1920s.

Similarly, cars or aeroplanes might now be possessed

for good or evil in the way humans or animals once were. The works of authors such as L.A. Lewis and Gerald Biss explore some of the opportunities available to the thoroughly modern supernatural entity.

Psychological fiction

The development of the psychological ghost story, as exemplified by writers such as Robert Hichens, Henry James and Oliver Onions, has proven to be of lasting literary worth.

The subtle atmospheric development essential to the creation of a satisfying ghostly tale seems uniquely suited to the psychological approach, while the change of focus from external threats to interior terrors of the mind allowed the ghost story to maintain its relevance in an increasingly materialistic era.

Some authors introduced a judicious use of ambiguity giving them considerable scope to create new perspectives on ghostly phenomena that were also open to rational interpretation. Sometimes, as with Henry James' celebrated *The Turn of the Screw* (1898), the reader is left to decide if the events depicted are supernatural or have more prosaic explanations.

However, much skill is needed to achieve this subtle uncertainty without confusing or frustrating the reader and few exponents of the psychological approach could consistently demonstrate such literary accomplishment. As a result, satisfactory examples of the psychological ghost story are rare, but include Robert Hichen's story *How Love Came to Professor Guildea*

(1900) and Oliver Onions' outstanding *The Rope in the Rafters* (1935).

Transformations

The werewolf legend spawned its own 'shapeshifting' sub-genre and remains an enduring theme together with the related and equally ancient idea of supernatural animals such as the phantom hound. However, there is much variation in the creatures mentioned in legends of human transformation, including those in Ovid's *Metamorphoses*.

Several highly publicised cases during the Middle Ages, most notably that of the Frenchman Gilles Garnier in 1574, fixed the idea of the werewolf or 'loup-garou' in European popular culture. Nineteenth century popularisers of 'true' ghost stories, such as Catherine Crowe, consolidated this lycanthropic tradition in works, including *Light and Darkness, or, Mysteries of Life* (1850), while stories such as George W.M. Reynolds' *Wagner, the Wehr-Wolf* (1857), Sir Gilbert Campbell's *The White Wolf of Kostopchin* (1889) and Guy Endore's famous *The Werewolf of Paris* (1933) further reinforced and elaborated the myth.

Over the years, writers have occasionally revisited the idea of animal transformation in stories whose subjects range from leopards to seagulls. Stevenson's *The Strange Case of Dr Jekyll and Mr Hyde* may be seen as a scientific variation of the idea. However, the predatory wolf man remains a favourite figure, only less powerful as an archetype than the most potent shapeshifting creation of all supernatural fiction: the vampire.

Vampires

The vampire sub-genre has become something of an industry in its own right, spawning numerous spin-off mythologies, merchandise and even themed nightclubs to cater for the vampire sub-culture.

The origins of the western vampire tradition can be traced back to antiquity with creatures such as the shapeshifting Empusae of Greek mythology and the biblical figure of Lilith. However, the vampire gained a new focus during the Middle Ages via a number of well-publicised cases of murder and blood-letting involving aristocrats, such as Countess Elizabeth Báthory and Gilles de Rais, as well as the infamous Vlad the Impaler, Dracul of Transylvania.

The concept of the aristocratic male vampire became a common motif in Gothic poetry. However, a significant step towards a recognisably modern vampire came with the publication of the first English language novel on the subject, *The Vampyre* (1819) by Lord Byron's physician, John Polidori. This seminal work heralded the transformation of the vampire from demon to doomed anti-hero by adding some of the more attractive characteristics of Polidori's patient, Lord Byron, into the already potent mix. This more romantic view of the vampire was fixed in the popular imagination through the creation of the huge and rambling 'penny dreadful' *Varney the Vampyre; or, The Feast of Blood* (1845-47) edited by J.M. Rymer.

Several writers returned to reinterpret the subject during the nineteenth century, most notably Sheridan Le Fanu in *Carmilla* (1872) and Sabine Baring-Gould in

Margery of Quether (1892). However, it was the publication of Bram Stoker's *Dracula* (1897) together with the emerging art of film-making that transformed the vampire myth into a sub-genre in its own right. A key reason for its success is that unlike other subjects, the complexity of the vampire myth allows it to stretch beyond the traditional supernatural short story format, providing enough material for full-length novels and films.

The ability of the vampire story to adapt to modern settings and interpretations has enabled it to permeate popular culture more easily than any other type of supernatural fiction. From the more traditional but updated novels of authors such as Ann Rice, through to the comic book and television activities of *Buffy the Vampire Slayer*, and full-scale science fiction reinterpretations such as Colin Wilson's *The Space Vampires* (1976), the sub-genre has proved a uniquely resilient and versatile form whose popularity shows no sign of diminishing. While subtle variations on the theme of 'psychic' vampirism have appeared over the years, the public's interest in the original bloodsucking monster of legend remains one of our strongest supernatural fascinations.

Neil Wilson 2014

Some Remarks on Ghost Stories by M.R. James

*Still, here you have a story written with
the sole object of inspiring a pleasing terror
in the reader; and as I think, that is the true aim
of the ghost story.*

This essay by the master ghost story writer M.R. James appeared in *The Bookman*, December 1929 (Christmas issue). *The Bookman* was a monthly magazine published in London from 1891 until 1934 by Hodder & Stoughton

Some Remarks on Ghost Stories

M.R. James

Very nearly all the ghost stories of old times claim to be true narratives of remarkable occurrences. At the outset I must make it clear that with these – be they ancient, mediaeval or post-mediaeval – I have nothing to do, any more than I have with those chronicled in our own days. I am concerned with a branch of fiction; not a large branch, if you look at the rest of the tree, but one which has been astonishingly fertile in the last thirty years. The avowedly fictitious ghost story is my subject, and that being understood I can proceed.

In the year 1854 George Borrow narrated to an audience of Welshmen, 'in the tavern of Gutter Vawr, in the county of Glamorgan', what he asserted to be 'decidedly the best ghost story in the world'. You may read this story either in English, in Knapp's notes to Wild Wales, or in Spanish, in a recent edition with excellent pictures (Las Aventuras de Pánfilo). The source is Lope de Vega's El Peregrino en so patria published in 1604. You will find it a remarkably interesting specimen of a tale of terror written in Shakespeare's lifetime, but I shall be surprised if you agree with Borrow's estimate of it. It is nothing but an account of a series of nightmares experienced by a wanderer who lodges for a night in a 'hospital', which had been deserted because of hauntings.

The ghosts come in crowds and play tricks with the victim's bed. They quarrel over cards, they squirt water at the man, they throw torches about the room. Finally they steal his clothes and disappear; but next morning the clothes are where he put them when he went to bed. In fact they are rather goblins than ghosts.

Still, here you have a story written with the sole object of inspiring a pleasing terror in the reader; and as I think, that is the true aim of the ghost story.

As far as I know, nearly two hundred years pass before you find the literary ghost story attempted again. Ghosts of course figure on the stage, but we must leave them out of consideration. Ghosts are the subject of quasi-scientific research in this country at the hands of Glanville, Beaumont and others; but these collectors are out to prove theories of the future life and the spiritual world. Improving treatises, with illustrative instances, are written on the Continent, as by Lavater. All these, if they do afford what our ancestors called amusement (Dr Johnson decreed that *Coriolanius* was 'amusing'), do so by a side-wind. The Castle of Otranto is perhaps the progenitor of the ghost story as a literary genre, and I fear that it is merely amusing in the modern sense.

Then we come to Mrs. Radcliffe, whose ghosts are far better of their kind, but with exasperating timidity are all explained away; and to Monk Lewis, who in the book which gives him his nickname is odious and horrible without being impressive. But Monk Lewis was responsible for better things than he could produce himself. It was under his auspices that Scott's verse first saw the light: among the Tales of Terror and Wonder are not only some of his translations, but 'Glenfinlas' and the 'Eve of St John', which must always rank as fine ghost stories. The form into which he cast them was that of the ballads which he loved and collected, and we must not forget that the ballad is in the direct line of ancestry of the ghost story. Think of 'Clerk Saunders', 'Young Benjie', the 'Wife of Usher's Well'. I am tempted to enlarge on the *Tales of Terror*, for the most part supremely absurd, where Lewis holds the pen, and jigs along with such stanzas as:

All present then uttered a terrified shout;
All turned with disgust from the scene.
The worms they crept in, and the worms they crept out,
And sported his eyes and his temples about,
While the spectre addressed Imogene.

But proportion must be observed.

If I were writing generally of horrific books which

include supernatural appearances, I would be obliged to include Maturin's *Melmoth*, and doubtless imitations of it which I know nothing of. But *Melmoth* is a long – a cruelly long – book, and we must keep our eye on the short prose ghost story in the first place. If Scott is not the creator of this, it is to him that we owe two classical specimens – 'Wandering Willie's Tale' and the 'Tapestried Chamber'. The former we know is an episode in a novel; anyone who searches the novels of succeeding years will certainly find (as we, alas, find in *Pickwick* and *Nicholas Nickleby*!) stories of this type foisted in; and possible some of them may be good enough to deserve reprinting.

But the real happy hunting ground, the proper habitat of our game is the magazine, the annual, the periodical publication destined to amuse the family circle. They came up thick and fast, the magazines, in the thirties and forties, and many died young. I do not, having myself sampled the task, envy the devoted one who sets out to examine the files, but it is not rash to promise him a measure of success. He will find ghost stories; but of what sort? Charles Dickens will tell us. In a paper from the Household Words, which will be found among 'Christmas Stories' under the name of 'A Christmas Tree' (I reckon it among the best of Dickens's occasional writings), that great man takes occasion to run through the plots of the typical ghost stories of his time.

As he remarks, they are 'reducible to a very few general types and classes; for ghosts have little originality, and "walk" in a beaten track.' He gives us at some length the experience of the nobleman and the ghost of the beautiful young housekeeper who drowned herself in the park two hundred years before; and more cursorily, the indelible bloodstain, the door that will not shut, the clock that strikes thirteen, the phantom coach, the compact to appear after death, the girl who meets her double, the cousin who is seen at the moment of his death far away in India, the maiden lady who 'really did see the Orphan Boy'. With such things as these we are still familiar. But we have rather forgotten – and I for my part have seldom met – those with which he ends his survey:

'Legion is the name of the German castles where we sit up alone to meet the spectre – where we are shown into a room made comparatively cheerful for our reception' (more detail, excellent of its kind, follows), 'and where, about the small hours of the night, we come into the knowledge of divers supernatural mysteries. Legion is the name of the haunted German students, in whose society we draw yet nearer to the fire, while the schoolboy in the corner opens his eyes wide and round, and flies off the footstool he has chosen for his seat, when the door accidentally blows open.'

As I have said, this German stratum of ghost stories is one of which I know little; but I am confident that the searcher of magazines will penetrate to it. Examples of the other types will accrue, especially when he reaches the era of Christmas Numbers, inaugurated by Dickens himself. His Christmas *Numbers* are not be confused with his Christmas *Books*, though the latter led on to the former. Ghosts are not absent from these, but I do not call the *Christmas Carol* a ghost story proper; while

I do assign that name to the stories of the Signalman and the Juryman (in 'Mugby Junction' and 'Dr Marigold').

These were written in 1865 and 1866, and nobody can deny that they conform to the modern idea of the ghost story. The setting and the personages are those of the writer's own day; they have nothing antique about them. Now this mode is not absolutely essential to success, but it is characteristic of the majority of successful stories: the belted knight who meets the spectre in the vaulted chamber and has to say 'By my halidom', or words to that effect, has little actuality about him. Anything, we feel might have happened in the 15th century. No; the seer of ghosts must talk something like me, and be dressed, if not in my fashion, yet not too much like a man in a pageant, if he is to enlist my sympathy. Wardour Street has no business here.

If Dickens's ghost stories are good and of the right complexion, they are not the best that were written in his day. The palm must I think be assigned to J.S. Le Fanu, whose stories of 'The Watcher' (or 'The Familiar'), 'Mr Justice Harbottle', 'Carmilla', are unsurpassed, while 'Schalken the Painter', Squire Toby's Will, the haunted house in 'The House by the Churchyard', 'Dickon the Devil', 'Madam Crowl's Ghost', run them very close. Is it the blend of French and Irish in Le Fanu's descent and surroundings that gives him the knack of infusing ominousness into his atmosphere? He is anyhow an artist in words; who else could have hit on the epithets in this sentence: 'The aerial image of the old house for a moment stood before her, with its peculiar malign, scared and skulking aspect.' Other famous stories of Le Fanu there are which are not quite ghosts stories – 'Green Tea' and 'The Room in the Dragon Volant'; and yet another, 'The Haunted Baronet', not famous, not even known but to a few, contains some admirable touches, but somehow lacks proportion. Upon mature consideration, I do not think that there are better ghost stories anywhere than the best of Le Fanu's; and among these I should give the first place to 'The Familiar' (alias 'The Watcher').

Other famous novelists of those days tried their hand – Bulwer Lytton for one. Nobody is permitted to write about ghost stories without mentioning 'The Haunters and the Haunted'. To my mind it is spoilt by the conclusion; the Cagliostro element (forgive an inaccuracy) is alien. It comes in with far better effect (though in a burlesque guise) in Thackeray's one attempt in this direction – 'The Notch in the Axe', in the 'Roundabout Papers'. This, to be sure, begins by being a skit partly on Dumas, partly on Lytton; but as Thackeray warmed to his work he got interested in the story and, as he says, was quite sorry to part with Pinto in the end. We have to reckon too with Wilkie Collins. 'The Haunted Hotel', a short novel, is by no means ineffective; grisly enough, almost, for the modern American taste.

Rhoda Broughton, Mrs. Riddell, Mrs. Henry Wood, Mrs. Oliphant – all these have some sufficiently absorbing stories to their credit.

I own to reading not infrequently 'Featherston's Story'

in the fifth series of 'Johnny Ludlow', to delighting in its domestic flavour and finding its ghost very convincing. (Johnny Ludlow, some young persons may not know, is by Mrs. Henry Wood.) The religious ghost story, as it may be called, was never done better than by Mrs. Oliphant in 'The Open Door' and 'A Beleaguered City'; though there is a competitor, and a strong one, in Le Fanu's 'Mysterious Lodger'.

Here I am conscious of a gap; my readers will have been conscious of many previous gaps. My memory does in fact slip on from Mrs. Oliphant to Marion Crawford and his horrid story of 'The Upper Berth', which (with the 'Screaming Skull' some distance behind) is the best in his collection of *Uncanny Tales*, and stands high among ghost stories in general.

That was I believe written in the late eighties. In the early nineties comes the deluge, the deluge of the illustrated monthly magazines, and it is no longer possible to keep pace with the output either of single stories or of volumes of collected ones. Never was the flow more copious than it is today, and it is only by chance that one comes across any given example. So nothing beyond scattering and general remarks can be offered. Some whole novels there have been which depend for all or part of their interest on ghostly matter. There is *Dracula*, which suffers by excess. (I fancy, by the way, that it must be based on a story in the fourth volume of Chambers's *Repository*, issued in the fifties.) There is 'Alice-for-Short', in which I never cease to admire the skill with which the ghost is woven into the web of the tale. But that is a very rare feat.

Among the collections of short stories, E.F. Benson's three volumes rank high, though to my mind he sins occasionally by stepping over the line of legitimate horridness. He is however blameless in this aspect as compared with some Americans, who compile volumes called *Not at Night* and the like. These are merely nauseating, and it is very easy to be nauseating. I, *moi qui vous parle*, could undertake to make a reader physically sick, if I chose to think and write in terms of the Grand Guignol. The authors of the stories I have in mind tread, as they believe, in the steps of Edgar Allen Poe and Ambrose Bierce (himself sometimes unpardonable), but they do not possess the force of either.

Reticence may be an elderly doctrine to preach, yet from the artistic point of view I am sure it is a sound one. Reticence conduces to effect, blatancy ruins it, and there is much blatancy in a lot of recent stories. They drag in sex too, which is a fatal mistake; sex is tiresome enough in the novels; in a ghost story, or as the backbone of a ghost story, I have no patience with it.

At the same time don't let us be mild and drab. Malevolence and terror, the glare of evil faces, 'the stony grin of unearthly malice', pursuing forms in darkness, and 'long-drawn, distant screams', are all in place, and so is a modicum of blood, shed with deliberation and carefully husbanded; the weltering and wallowing that I too often encounter merely recall the methods of M.G. Lewis.

Clearly it is out of the question for me to begin upon a series of 'short notices' of recent collections; but an illustrative instance or two will be to the point. A.M. Burrage, in *Some Ghost Stories*, keeps on the right side of the line, and if about half of his ghosts are amiable, the rest have their terrors, and no mean ones. H.R. Wakefield, in *They Return at Evening* (a good title), gives us a mixed bag, from which I should remove one or two that leave a nasty taste. Among the residue are some admirable pieces, very inventive.

Going back a few years I light on Mrs. Everett's *The Death Mask*, of rather quieter tone on the whole, but with some excellently conceived stories. Hugh Benson's *Light Invisible* and *Mirror of Shalott* are too ecclesiastical. K. and Hesketh Prichard's *Flaxman Low* is most ingenious and successful, but rather over-technically 'occult'. It seems impertinent to apply the same criticism to Algernon Blackwood, but *John Silence* is surely open to it. Mr. Eliot O'Donnell's multitudinous volumes I do not know whether to class as narratives of fact or exercises in fiction. I hope they may be of the latter sort, for life in a world managed by his gods and infested by his demons seems a risky business.

So I might go on through a long list of authors; but the remarks one can make in an article of this compass can hardly be illuminating. The reading of many ghost stories has shown me that the greatest successes have been scored by the authors who can make us envisage a definite time and place., and give us plenty of clear-cut and matter-of-fact detail, but who, when the climax is reached, allow us to be just a little in the dark as to the working of their machinery. We do not want to see the bones of their theory about the supernatural.

All this while I have confined myself almost entirely to the English ghost story. The fact is that either there are not many good stories by foreign writers, or (more probably) my ignorance has veiled them from me. But I should feel myself ungrateful if I did not pay a tribute to the supernatural tales of Erckman-Chatrian. The blend of French with German in them, comparable to the French-Irish blend in Le Fanu, has produced some quite first-class romance of this kind. Among longer stories, *La Maison Forestiere* (and, if you will, *Hugues le loup*); among shorter ones Le Blanc et le noir, Le Reve du cousin Elof and L'OEil invisible have for years delighted and alarmed me. It is high time that they were made more accessible than they are.

There need not be any peroration to a series of rather disjointed reflections. I will only ask the reader to believe that, though I have not hitherto mentioned it, I have read *The Turn of the Screw*.

M.R. James

M.R. James: Readings and TV Adaptations

M.R. James (1862-1936) was Provost of King's College, Cambridge, and Eton. (See separate entry in this volume on this master ghost story writer.) He read many of his stories to select gatherings of friends at King's College in the early twentieth century.

These atmospheric occasions have been beautifully captured by two very different actors: Christopher Lee (who met James while a schoolboy at Eton), and more recently, Robert Lloyd Parry. In the *Fortean Times* magazine, September 2012, Parry wrote: '*...for most people, 150 years after he was born, 78 years after he died, James' words and tales still have the power to transfix.*'

Also well worth watching are the 1970s BBC adaptations of a number of James' ghost stories under the umbrella heading, *A Ghost Story for Christmas*, productions which are still much admired today.

Masters of the Ghost Story Genre

Introduction

The authors featured here are among the ghost story genre's finest exponents. They include M.R. James, widely acknowledged as the master of classic ghost fiction, as well as other familiar names such as Mrs Gaskell, Charles Dickens, Wilkie Collins and Henry James.

Less well-known authors, also hugely admired by ghost story aficionados, include Oliver Onions, whose work was characterised by subtlety and a rare psychological insight; Mrs J.H. Riddell who helped to define the archetypal Victorian ghost story; and H.R. Wakefield, whose first two volumes of highly acclaimed ghost stories were thought to rival those of M.R. James.

DB

E.F. Benson (1867-1940)

Edward Frederic Benson was the second member of the eccentric trio of Benson brothers. Born in Wokingham, Berkshire, Benson was educated at Marlborough College and Cambridge University where he achieved a first in classics. Following his early academic success, Benson spent a number of years working in Greece and Egypt pursuing his antiquarian interests.

He returned to England with the firm intention of becoming a writer and gained considerable acclaim for his first novel *Dodo* (1893), a work which marked the beginning of a prolific and commercially rewarding literary career. During his long life, Benson published over 100 books on a variety of subjects, although the majority were works of fiction. Benson is best remembered for the popular Mapp and Lucia series of social comedies that began with *Queen Lucia* in 1920.

Benson contributed regularly to periodicals, with many of his ghost stories first appearing in the popular *Hutchinson's Magazine*. Several of these tales are set in or around Rye in Sussex, where Benson lived at Lamb House, a property formerly occupied by the writer Henry James, who was a family friend. It was in the garden at Lamb House that Benson, who had a keen interest in the supernatural, once claimed to have seen a ghost. Benson eventually became Mayor of Rye from 1934 to 1937.

While all three of the Benson brothers wrote ghost stories, it is generally acknowledged that E. F. Benson made the most significant contribution to the genre. He was present at several of M.R. James' celebrated ghost story readings at Cambridge University and it is possible that this inspired him to attempt his own macabre works.

However, unlike James' subtle supernatural protagonists, Benson's ghosts frequently manifest in a more physical way and range from repulsive creatures to mutilated figures capable of inflicting both physical and spiritual harm on their unfortunate victims. Elements of sadism and misogyny are clearly detectable in several stories, with women depicted as evil figures preying upon weak men or as victims suffering cruel fates at the hands of demonic tormentors.

Benson also produced several novels with strong supernatural elements, however these are not as successful as his shorter works in the genre. While his short stories sometimes suffer from hurried execution, the overall quality is high and many are notable for their originality and effect.

Selected bibliography

The Judgment Books by E.F. Benson. London: Osgood, McIlvaine & Co., 1895.
An early novel about the evil influence exerted by an old family portrait.

The Room in the Tower and Other Stories by E.F. Benson. London: Mills & Boon Limited, 1912.
Benson's first collection of original and well-crafted ghost stories. Several tales, including the title work, have become anthology standards.

Visible and Invisible by E.F. Benson. London: Hutchinson and Co., 1923.
A highly sought after work which is arguably Benson's best general short story collection. The book includes several of the author's most frequently anthologised tales. However, despite its promising title, the tale And the Dead Spake is closer to science fiction or horror than the supernatural.

Spook Stories by E.F. Benson. London: Hutchinson & Co (Publishers) Ltd., 1928.
A further high quality collection of Benson's ghostly contributions

to Hutchinson's Magazine. A classic of the genre.

Ravens' Brood by E.F. Benson. London: Arthur Barker Limited, 1934.
A witchcraft novel set in the English countryside. Better than many of Benson's other supernatural novels, but still not up to the standard of his short stories.

Algernon Blackwood (1869-1951)

Algernon Henry Blackwood is widely acknowledged as one of the genre's most important writers and was admired by such diverse masters of supernatural fiction as M.R. James and H.P. Lovecraft

Born into a wealthy middle-class English family, Blackwood was educated at a school of the Moravian Brotherhood in Germany's Black Forest. Rebelling against his strict religious upbringing, Blackwood followed a similar path to members of the later hippy generation, studying both eastern mysticism and western occultism before being packed off to Canada in 1890 by his disappointed family. Details of many of the formative experiences gained during his travels in Canada and the USA are related in his autobiography, *Episodes Before Thirty* (1923).

Blackwood returned to England in 1899 and continued his occult studies, becoming a member of the foremost English occult group of the period, the Golden Dawn. It is notable that many other writers of supernatural material, including Arthur Machen, Bram Stoker and the notorious Aleistair Crowley, were also members of the Golden Dawn during this period and drew upon the experience in their works.

Diversity characterised Blackwood's long life. Before starting his writing career, he tried a wide range of jobs including bartender, artists' model, and farmer. Even after he achieved literary success, Blackwood still found time to work as an actor and even a secret agent. It was, however, as a broadcaster that he became a household name. From 1934, working in both radio and television as the BBC's 'Ghost Man', he introduced a new generation to supernatural fiction, receiving a CBE for his contribution to the media in 1949.

During his life, Blackwood published more than 200 stories, novels, plays and essays, many supernatural in content. His first ghost story, *A Haunted Island*, appeared in 1898. Blackwood's prodigious output also included many works of fantasy, humour and mysticism, with one children's story, *A Prisoner in Fairyland*, being adapted for the stage in 1915 as *The Starlight Express* with music by Sir Edward Elgar. Blackwood was at the height of his powers during the decade 1906-1916 when many of his best ghost stories were written.

Paradoxically, one strength of Blackwood's writing – his passionate belief in the reality of the supernatural – can also be considered its greatest weakness. His supernatural protagonists are not usually the spectral human ghosts of Charles Dickens or Sheridan Le Fanu, but more commonly impersonal and elemental forces of nature, blind to human morality and self-importance. This is largely because Blackwood used his fiction not simply to entertain, but to promote his mystical beliefs more widely. This gives his work moments of great atmospheric intensity, though many are then spoilt by verbose and over technical explanations of occult theory.

Many of Blackwood's tales were republished in a variety of collections even during his lifetime. *The Tales of Algernon Blackwood* (London: Martin Secker, 1938) is the author's own selection of his favourite stories; the autobiographical introduction sheds new light on their inspiration and composition.

Selected bibliography

The Empty House and Other Ghost Stories by Algernon Blackwood. London: Eveleigh Nash, 1906.
Originally sent to the publishers by a friend, Blackwood's first collection of stories includes several based on his own experiences in America and Canada. The book was well-received and encouraged Blackwood to pursue a literary career. It is now regarded as a classic.

The Listener and Other Stories by Algernon Blackwood. London: Eveleigh Nash, 1907.
This collection contains some of Blackwood's best work, most notably The Willows, *arguably the best single supernatural story in the genre.*

John Silence, Physician Extraordinary by Algernon Blackwood. London: Eveleigh Nash, 1908.
Blackwood's contribution to the occult detective sub-genre was originally intended as a non-fiction work detailing the author's experiences of the occult. The book's dedication is: 'To M.L.W. the original of John Silence and my companion in many adventures'.

Shocks by Algernon Blackwood. London: Grayson & Grayson, 1935.
Blackwood's last major collection. The quality is variable, with more than one tale touching on the subject of suicide.

Wilkie Collins (1824-1889)

William Wilkie Collins was born in London, the son of a successful artist. Although Collins studied for the Bar, he never joined the legal profession, preferring to concentrate on a writing career. However, his first novel, *Antonina* (1850), received poor reviews and proved to be his last attempt at historical fiction.

Collins developed a close professional relationship with fellow author Charles Dickens, eventually becoming editor of Dickens' *Household Words* magazine. The two men also collaborated on several stories but, as is common with such works, these were not as artistically successful as their individual efforts.

Collins gradually developed a reputation for well-crafted and highly ingenious mystery novels of which *The Moonstone* (1868) and *The Woman in White* (1860) are the best known today. The structure and style of these sophisticated works laid many of the foundations for the crime and thriller fiction genres. While Collins' greatest strength is his ability to construct imaginative and well-paced plots, his works are also notable for their fine characterisation and attention to background detail.

His suspense novels sometimes incorporate supernatural features and in common with many contributors to Charles Dickens' magazines, he also wrote a number of short ghost stories that share the fine qualities of his mystery novels.

One common theme in Collins' crime and supernatural fiction is a strong sense of outrage at injustice. His detectives correct this moral imbalance in his novels while his ghosts act as catalysts for retribution in his supernatural tales.

A further similarity is the exploration of individual reactions to the emotion of fear, whether induced by supernatural dread or sheer physical horror.

Throughout his life, Collins suffered periodic bouts of ill health and in common with many contemporaries, including Queen Victoria, this led to an increasing dependence on the opium derivative, laudanum. His later work suffered because of this addiction and his final stories are of a considerably lower standard than his novels of the 1860s.

Nevertheless, there is still much for the supernatural fiction enthusiast to discover among Collins' early work. While a few of his tales have been regularly anthologised, excellent novels such as *Armadale* (1866) have been largely passed over in favour of his better known works.

Selected bibliography

The Queen of Hearts by Wilkie Collins, in Three Volumes. London: Hurst and Blackett Publishers, Successors to Henry Colburn, 1859.
A general collection of linked stories, two of which have

supernatural features: Brother Morgan's Story of the Dream-Woman *is a longer version of* The Ostler *which appeared in the 1855 Christmas number of* Household Words. *The story has been frequently reprinted as* The Dream Woman *or* Alicia Warlock. Brother Griffith's Story of Mad Monkton *originally appeared in* Fraser's Magazine *as* The Monktons of Wincot Abbey *and is usually anthologised as* Mad Monkton.

Armadale by Wilkie Collins with Twenty Illustrations by George H. Thomas in Two Volumes. London: Smith, Elder & Co., 1866.
An excellent mystery novel with strong supernatural features. Sophisticated and intricately constructed.

The Best Supernatural Stories of Wilkie Collins Selected and Introduced by Peter Haining. London: Robert Hale, 1990.
A good selection of Collins' macabre work which includes some rare material such as The Ostler, *the original version of Collins' celebrated story,* The Dream Woman. The Dead Hand *consists of chapter two of Collins' collaborative work with Charles Dickens,* The Lazy Tour of Two Idle Apprentices. John Jago's Ghost *is a crime story that rationalises seemingly supernatural events.*

Walter de la Mare (1873-1956)

Walter de la Mare was born at Charlton in Kent and educated at St Paul's School in London. He contributed several short stories to magazines in the late 1890s while working for an oil company, but recognition of his talents did not come until the publication of a volume of poems, *Songs of Childhood,* in

1902. A civil pension awarded in 1906 finally allowed de la Mare to concentrate solely on his writing and from this time he produced a steady and varied stream of essays, poetry and fiction for adults and children.

Compiling a definitive list of de la Mare's work is complicated by several factors. In common with many other authors, much of his work first appeared in periodicals with some early pieces under pseudonyms. More unusually, however, de la Mare's desire for perfection often led him to revise works quite substantially over time, with new editions of novels such as *The Return* (1910) appearing throughout his life.

The author's short stories were also repackaged in a variety of collections, regularly combining new and previously published material. In addition, many works were originally produced in limited editions with specially commissioned illustrations. His post as an executive at the publisher Faber and Faber doubtless assisted in these bibliographic variations.

Although de la Mare's first supernatural tale, *Kismet*, was published in magazine form in 1895, he did not write regularly in the genre until the 1920s. A fascination with the mysterious and the magical permeates much of de la Mare's work. His children's stories are colourful fantasy tales of great vigour with a clear moral stance, while his adult fiction shares with his poetry an ambiguous dreamlike quality coupled with a subtle and lyrical beauty.

His exploration of the relationships between the everyday world, the magical and the macabre was highly original and made a significant contribution to the supernatural genre.

Selected bibliography

The Return by Walter de la Mare. London: Edward Arnold, 1910.
A well-written and subtle metaphysical novel about evil possession. The story is written in a slightly different style from de la Mare's other macabre work. Revised editions of the novel were published in 1922 (London: W. Collins Sons & Co. Ltd) and 1945 (London: Faber and Faber).

The Riddle and Other Stories by Walter de la Mare. London: Selwyn & Blount Limited, 1923.
A general collection, including one of de la Mare's best-known supernatural short stories, Seaton's Aunt. *This story was reprinted in London by Faber & Gwyer in 1927 with a wood-engraving on the front cover by Blair Hughes-Stanton.*

The Connoisseur and Other Stories by Walter de la Mare. London: W. Collins Sons & Co. Ltd., 1926.
A mainstream collection which includes de la Mare's best-known and most effective ghost story, All Hallows. *The story,* Mr Kemp, *is a rather ambiguous horror tale which has sometimes been included in supernatural fiction anthologies.*

They Walk Again: An Anthology of Ghost Stories Chosen by Colin de La Mare with an Introduction by Walter de la Mare. London: Faber & Faber Limited, 1931.
A collection of ghost stories assembled by de la Mare's son that includes an interesting introduction by Walter de la Mare as well as his popular story, All Hallows.

The Wind Blows Over by Walter de la Mare. London: Faber and Faber Limited, 1936.

A wonderful collection of de la Mare's supernatural and fantasy tales. A limited edition of seventy-five numbered copies on handmade paper was issued later in the same month.

Charles Dickens (1812-1870)

Charles Dickens was born in the naval town of Portsmouth where his father worked in the Royal Navy's pay department. His education was disrupted by his family's moves to Chatham, Kent, and eventually London, where financial problems led to his father being sent to debtor's prison.

Dickens first worked as an articled clerk in a lawyer's office before joining the prestigious *Morning Chronicle* as a reporter. The series of magazine articles he wrote during this early period were later collected as *Sketches by Boz* (1836). It was on the strength of this work that Dickens was commissioned to write *The Posthumous Papers of the Pickwick Club*, which appeared in serial form from 1837. In the same year, he became editor of the periodical *Bentley's Miscellany*. *The Pickwick Papers* established his reputation and he went on to write a string of successful novels, including *Nicholas Nickleby* (1838), *Martin Chuzzlewit* (1844) and *Bleak House* (1853).

During his lifetime, Dickens was editor and proprietor of several successful magazines, including *Household Words* (1850-1859) and *All the Year Round* (1859-1870). In addition to his own work, these magazines frequently contained contributions from other notable authors of the period, including Mrs Gaskell and

Wilkie Collins. Dickens was an amazingly prolific author; the volume and quality of his output is all the more impressive considering the tight commercial deadlines he was forced to meet.

While aspects of Dickens' work may now seem sentimental and melodramatic, he was completely in tune with contemporary public taste and enormously popular both in Britain and America. In some respects, he acted as the conscience of Victorian society, his sympathetic portrayals of poverty and hardship owing much to his own childhood experiences. A master storyteller, Dickens was also a gifted reader of his own work, and travelled widely giving dramatic readings to appreciative audiences. A combination of overwork and extensive travelling almost certainly contributed to Dickens' early death in 1870.

As a child, Dickens had been introduced to the supernatural through the tales of his nurse-maid, Mary Weller. He was also an avid reader of the popular 'penny dreadfuls' which regularly chronicled horrific and ghostly events. Dickens' interest in the macabre continued throughout his life and he incorporated aspects of the supernatural and grotesque into several of his mainstream novels, including *Nicholas Nickleby*, *The Pickwick Papers,* and in particular, *Bleak House,* which includes a description of spontaneous human combustion.

The publication of one of Dickens' most enduringly popular works, *A Christmas Carol* (1843), began the association of Christmas with supernatural tales, and he encouraged other authors to write ghost stories for the Christmas numbers of his magazines; this cemented the link between the festive and the ghostly in popular culture – a tradition which continues today.

In addition to the more famous *A Christmas Carol*, Dickens also produced a similar moralistic dream fantasy, *The Chimes* (1844), sections of which have occasionally appeared in anthologies of supernatural or fantasy fiction.

Dickens' ghost fiction ranges from the humorous to the horrific and, in common with much of his other work, frequently delivers a moral message.

While he produced relatively few supernatural stories, Dickens' encouragement of serious authors to attempt ghostly fiction was a crucial factor in transforming the ghost story from a pulp genre to a respectable literary form, laying the foundations for the golden age of Victorian supernatural writing.

Selected bibliography

Charles Dickens' Christmas Ghost Stories Selected and Introduced by Peter Haining. London: Robert Hale, 1992.
An excellent collection of Dickens' supernatural tales, most of which were published in the Christmas editions of All the Year Round *and* Household Words magazines. *The anthology includes Dickens' essay on spiritualism,* Ghosts and Ghost-Seers *together with his satire on the same subject,* The Rapping Spirits.

The Complete Ghost Stories of Charles Dickens Edited and Introduced by Peter Haining. London: Michael Joseph, 1982.

The most comprehensive collection of Dickens' supernatural stories together with a detailed critical introduction by the ghost story anthologist Peter Haining. The work includes two anonymous items: Four Ghost Stories *and* The Portrait Painter's Story, *from* All the Year Round *which Haining believes are by Dickens.*

Extracts from Household Words, relating to Mr. C. Dickens' visit to Lancaster; with extracts from the Official Illustrated Guide of the Lancaster & Carlisle, Caledonian and Edinburgh & Glasgow Railways; also, description of the torch-light procession in Lancaster, on the marriage of H.R.H. the Prince of Wales, March 10th 1863. Lancaster: printed by G.C. Clark, Gazette Office, 1866.

A collaboration with Wilkie Collins (see separate entry on this author). Included in chapter four is a self-contained ghost story which has been reprinted under the title The Ghost and the Bridal Chamber.

The Posthumous Papers of the Pickwick Club by Charles Dickens with Forty-Three Illustrations by R. Seymour and Phiz. London: Chapman & Hall, 1837.

Humorous work that established Dickens' literary reputation. Includes several self-contained supernatural tales: The Lawyer and the Ghost, The Queer Chair, The Ghosts of the Mail, A Madman's Manuscript *and* The Story of the Goblins Who Stole a Sexton.

The Life and Adventures of Nicholas Nickleby. London: Chapman & Hall, 1839.

A mainstream novel that includes a self-contained supernatural tale, Baron Koëldwethout's Apparition.

A Christmas Carol in Prose: Being a Ghost-Story of Christmas by Charles Dickens with Illustrations by John Leech. London: Chapman & Hall, 1843.
One of Dickens' most successful works and certainly the most popular ghost story ever written. A section of the work has also been anthologised under the titles Marley's Ghost *and* Old Marley's Ghost.

Mrs Gaskell (1810-1865)

Elizabeth Cleghorn Stevenson was born in London but following the early death of her mother was brought up in Knutsford, Cheshire, by an aunt. At the age of 21, she married William Gaskell, a Unitarian minister, and went to live with him in the industrial city of Manchester. Encouraged by her husband, Gaskell began to write, at first in collaboration with him and later on her own.

After several years of writing short magazine pieces, literary success came in 1848 with the publication of her novel *Mary Barton*. Charles Dickens was impressed by Gaskell's work, and invited her to contribute material to his popular magazine *Household Words*. Much of Gaskell's work, including the celebrated novel *Cranford* (1853), made its first appearance in the magazine. During this period, Gaskell became friends with the writer Charlotte Brontë and later wrote a classic biography of her fellow novelist.

Gaskell's supernatural fiction ranks among the best of

the Victorian period, with several of her most famous tales, including *The Old Nurse's Story* (1852) and *The Squire's Story* (1853), originally appearing in Christmas issues of *Household Words*. Gaskell's ghost tales are scattered throughout various periodicals and books of short stories and no single volume collection existed until 1978 when Michael Ashley produced *Mrs Gaskell's Tales of Mystery and Horror*.

Together with Dickens' work, Gaskell's ghost fiction helped consolidate the association of the supernatural tale with the Victorian Christmas. Gaskell claimed to have seen a ghost and her belief in their reality may have added an extra dimension to her macabre writing. However, the main reason for her success is the combination of superb narrative technique and skilled control of atmosphere.

An additional reason for the popularity of Gaskell's supernatural work during the Victorian period is its lack of moral ambiguity. While some modern readers might find this moralistic standpoint a little simplistic, there is no doubting the effectiveness of Gaskell's writing. Most of her ghost stories are as enjoyable today as when they first appeared.

Selected bibliography

Round the Sofa by the Author of 'Mary Barton', 'Life of Charlotte Brontë', &c. &c., Two Volumes. London: Sampson Low, Son & Co., 1859.
A series of linked stories told in Margaret Dawson's sitting room in Edinburgh. The work includes The Doom of the Griffiths *which was Gaskell's first ghost story and* The Poor Clare *about the effects of a curse.*

Right at Last and Other Tales by the Author of 'Mary Barton', 'Life of Charlotte Brontë', 'Round the Sofa' &c. London: Sampson Low, Son & Co., 1860.

The first book appearance of Lois the Witch *which had appeared in periodical form in* All the Year Round *during the previous year. An illustrated edition of Gaskell's short witchcraft novel was published in 1960 in London by Methuen, with pictures by Faith Jaques.*

The Grey Woman and Other Tales by Mrs Gaskell. London: Smith Elder & Co., 1865.

A mainstream collection of stories containing the supernatural tale, Curious if True

William Hope Hodgson (1877-1918)

William Hope Hodgson was born at Blackmore End, Essex, the son of an impoverished Anglican clergyman. From an early age he was fascinated by all things nautical and attempted to run away to sea while still a child; he was soon caught and forced to return home.

Hodgson's ambition to become a sailor was finally realised in 1891 and he spent the next eight years at sea, gaining the experiences he would later use in much of his popular fiction. At sea, Hodgson became an early convert to the new 'science' of body building and published his theories on the subject in a series of magazine articles.

The success of these pieces encouraged Hodgson to try writing fiction and his short story *The Goddess of Kali* was published in 1904. This was followed by a series of seaborne macabre and mystery stories culminating with Hodgson's novel *The Boats of the Glen Carrig* (1907) and he continued to write mainstream sea adventures for several more years.

At the same time, he began experimenting with the supernatural and science fiction genres, producing highly unusual and influential works such as *The House on the Borderland* (1908) and *The Night Land* (1912).

Although Hodgson was not a great prose stylist, he had a remarkably vivid imagination and became highly skilled at the evocation of macabre atmospheres. Despite his unfamiliarity with psychic research, Hodgson's occult detective character, Thomas Carnacki, was convincing enough to become an enduring favourite among ghost story enthusiasts and received the rare accolade of a pastiche collection, *No. 472 Cheyne Walk* (1992) by A. F. (Chico) Kidd and Rick Kennett.

Hodgson was killed in action during the First World War and one can only speculate on where his remarkable imagination might have led had he survived.

Although the popularity of Hodgson's stories diminished in Britain during the 1920s, he developed a cult following in the United States, where the cosmic scale of his work appealed to a new generation of readers looking for something beyond traditional haunted house tales.

Hodgson's novels strongly influenced the work of H.P. Lovecraft and his followers and helped shape their 'science fiction Gothic' style of supernatural writing. Hodgson's reputation has grown steadily on both sides of the Atlantic since the 1960s when he was rediscovered by a new generation of readers eager to explore the extremes of human experience.

Most of Hodgson's works have been reprinted and useful new critical appraisals have appeared. Sam Moskowitz's collection of Hodgson's rarest short stories, *Out of the Storm* (1975), published in the United States only, is particularly noteworthy for its fascinating biographical introduction to Hodgson's life and work.

Selected bibliography

Carnacki, the Ghost Finder and a Poem by William Hope Hodgson. London: c1910.
The earliest appearance of Hodgson's celebrated supernatural sleuth.

Carnacki the Ghost-Finder by William Hope Hodgson. London: Eveleigh Nash, 1913.
A classic collection of short stories firmly in the occult detective sub-genre. Although poorly constructed technically, Hodgson's vivid imagination produces convincing suspense and supernatural horror. The work was later republished in the United States (Sauk City, Wis.: Mycroft & Moran, 1947) with an additional tale, The Hog, which some claim is a Hodgson pastiche by the author and anthologist August Derleth.

The House on the Borderland: from the manuscript, discovered in 1877 by Messrs. Tonnison and Berreggnog, in the ruins that lie to the south of the village of Kraighten, in the west of Ireland, set out here with notes by William Hope Hodgson. London:

Chapman and Hall Ltd., 1908.
A highly influential, innovative and imaginative novel about the experiences of the unfortunate occupant of an ancient Irish house besieged by malevolent supernatural forces.

The Ghost Pirates by William Hope Hodgson with a frontispiece by Sidney H. Sime. London: Stanley Paul & Co., 1909.
Arguably Hodgson's most artistically successful supernatural novel combines a realistic depiction of sea life with a solidly constructed and highly original plot. A revised version of the novel's original ending has been anthologised as The Silent Ship.

Henry James (1843-1916)

Henry James was born in New York, but raised and educated mainly in Europe, a continent he came to regard as his spiritual home. James returned to America in 1860 to study law at Harvard University but found literature more appealing than the legal profession and soon began to submit short stories to magazines in the hope of becoming a professional writer. His first success came with the publication of *The Story of a Year* in the *Atlantic Monthly* in 1865 and this began a long association with the periodical. In 1869 James emigrated to England where he remained for the rest of his life, finally becoming a British citizen in 1915.

James' first novel *Watch and Ward* was published in 1871 but it was not until *Roderick Hudson* (1875) that his work began to receive significant critical attention. The next decade was arguably the most artistically successful of James' career with major works, including

Daisy Miller (1878), *Washington Square* (1880) and *Portrait of a Lady* (1881), appearing in rapid succession. Many of the author's novels explore the changing relationship between American and European society at a time when the power of the New World was beginning to eclipse that of the old.

James' work was less commercially successful during the 1890s, although by this time he had developed a considerable reputation amongst both writers and critics as a master prose stylist. After an ill-fated attempt at writing drama, success returned in 1897 with a novel, *The Awkward Age*. A year later, James produced what would come to be regarded by many as one of the greatest supernatural stories ever written: *The Turn of the Screw*.

James had already written several ghost stories during his career and after a number of more conventional early tales developed a subtle and thought-provoking style of supernatural writing that was uniquely his. Several influences were important in James' 'interior' approach to the uncanny, but probably most significant were the theories of his brother, William James, the famous psychologist, who had made a detailed study of human reactions to religion and the supernatural.

The particular inspiration for *The Turn of the Screw* came from an anecdote related by Archbishop Benson, father of the three Benson brothers mentioned elsewhere in this volume. James reworked Benson's tale extensively, emphasising one of his favourite themes – possession of an individual by evil forces –

and succeeded in creating a masterpiece which has fascinated and horrified readers since it was first published. The story has been adapted for a variety of media, being filmed as *The Innocents* (1961) and turned into an opera by Benjamin Britten in 1954. Ironically, the work's reception seems to have surprised and puzzled James who regarded it as something of a potboiler. In 1997, Hilary Bailey wrote a sequel, *Miles and Flora*.

James continued to write occasionally in the ghost genre for the rest of his life, although he never again created a piece to rival the power of *The Turn of the Screw*. An attempt to write a full-length supernatural novel foundered and the incomplete manuscript was published posthumously as *The Sense of the Past* (1917).

Although sometimes criticised for his perceived verbosity and overcomplicated literary style, James' reputation continued to grow in the years following his death and he is now regarded as one of the most significant figures of modern English literature. The quality of James' supernatural writing assures him of equal stature among writers of the genre.

Selected bibliography

Stories Revived: In Three Volumes by Henry James. London: Macmillan and Co., 1885.
A general collection of short stories, including some supernatural tales such as The Romance of Certain Old Clothes *which are written in a more traditional style than James' later work.*

The Lesson of the Master: The Marriages, The Pupil, Brooksmith, The Solution, Sir Edmund Orme by

Henry James. London and New York: Macmillan and Co., 1892.

A general collection, including one of James' most anthologised ghost stories, Sir Edmund Orme, *the first of his supernatural stories to be written from a psychological viewpoint.*

The Private Life: The Wheel of Time, Lord Beaupre, The Visits, Collaboration, Owen Wingrave by Henry James. London: James R. Osgood, McIlvaine & Co., 1893.

A general collection, including one of James' most interesting macabre stories, Owen Wingrave.

Embarrassments: The Figure in the Carpet, Glasses, The Next Time, The Way it Came by Henry James. London: William Heinemann, 1896.

This work has also been reprinted as The Friends of the Friends.

The Two Magics: The Turn of the Screw, Covering End by Henry James. London: William Heinemann, 1898.

Two novella-length tales, one of which is James' supernatural masterpiece, The Turn of the Screw: *arguably the greatest psychological ghost story ever written.*

The Soft Side by Henry James. London: Methuen & Co., 1900.

An excellent mainstream short story collection containing some first-class ghostly tales. James at his very best.

The Better Sort by Henry James. London: Methuen & Co., 1903.

A general collection, including the psychological ghost story, The Beast in the Jungle, *a work considered by some to be James' greatest short story achievement.*

In After Days: Thoughts on the Future Life by W.D. Howells, Henry James, John Bigelow, Thomas Wentworth Higginson, Henry M. Alden, William Hanna Thomson, Guglielmo Ferrero, Julia Ward Howe, Elizabeth Stuart Phelps, with portraits. New York & London: Harper & Brothers Publishers, 1910. *The chapter by Henry James is entitled,* Is There a Life After Death?

M.R. James (1862-1936)

Montague Rhodes James was born at Goodnestone, Kent, and educated at Eton and King's College, Cambridge. A keen antiquarian, he pursued a highly successful academic career after graduation, becoming a Fellow of King's in 1887 and then Provost in 1905. He also served as a director of Cambridge's Fitzwilliam Museum.

James was an expert bibliophile, responsible for the production of catalogues of several previously unrecorded college collections of rare books and manuscripts as well as *A List of Manuscripts Formerly Owned by Dr John Dee* (1921), a catalogue of the library of the infamous Elizabethan occultist and spy.

In addition to his scholarly works, James wrote a number of more accessible publications, including *Old Testament Legends* (1913) and a historical guide to two English counties, *Norfolk and Suffolk* (1930). During vacations, he travelled widely in Northern Europe and later used his experiences in his ghost fiction. James returned to his beloved Eton in 1918 as its Provost, and remained there until his death in 1936.

Although he was somewhat ambiguous about his personal belief in ghosts, James was a keen reader of supernatural fiction and a particular admirer of the works of the French writers, Émile Erckmann and Alexandre Chatrian (nearly all of whose works were jointly written) and the Irish author, Sheridan Le Fanu.

James was so impressed by Le Fanu's work that he eventually assembled a collection of the author's rarest macabre stories, *Madam Crowl's Ghost* in 1923. He was also inspired to write his own ghost stories and in 1893 read his first tales, *Canon Alberic's Scrap-Book* and *Lost Hearts*, to a small but appreciative audience of friends and colleagues. This event began a tradition of ghost story readings at King's that helped inspire several of those present, including E.F. Benson, to write their own supernatural fiction.

James' earliest supernatural work was collected in the seminal *Ghost Stories of an Antiquary* (1904), a work that set the benchmark for ghost fiction for the next fifty years. It is indicative of James' considerable popular influence that he was commissioned to write a story for inclusion in the miniature library of Queen Mary's doll's house. James also became an acknowledged expert on the subject of supernatural literature and contributed several articles to books and journals on the topic.

James' ghost stories closely mirror his own interests and lifestyle and frequently feature bachelor academics whose excessive scholastic curiosity leads them into dangerous supernatural encounters that challenge their rationalist beliefs.

The author's profound historical knowledge lends his stories the convincing background detail essential for the suspension of disbelief and the creation of a successful ghostly atmosphere.

A particular trademark of James' writing, which demonstrates his debt to Le Fanu in particular, is his highly subtle but measured introduction of ghostly events into narratives which build slowly but inexorably to a horrific climax. However, an effective counterpoint to the increasingly dark events of some of James' narratives is his occasional but judicious use of whimsical humour.

Many years after his death, James still inspires imitators who attempt to capture the antiquarian flavour of his work and numerous tales continue to be adapted for radio and television, particularly for Christmas broadcasts. In 1993, the Ghost Story Press published a facsimile reprint of James' first tales, *Two Ghost Stories: A Centenary*, with an introduction by his biographer Michael Cox.

Although James produced relatively few tales in comparison to some other authors in the genre, his reputation and influence remain undiminished and he continues to be regarded by many as the undisputed master of the English ghost story.

Selected bibliography

Ghost Stories of an Antiquary by Montague Rhodes James with Four Illustrations by the late James McBryde. London: Edward Arnold, 1904.
A seminal collection of traditional English ghost stories which has been much imitated but never fully equalled.

More Ghost Stories of an Antiquary by Montague Rhodes James. London: Edward Arnold, 1911.
A further excellent collection of classic ghost fiction. An uncompleted early draft of the story Mr Humphreys and his Inheritance *was later published in* Ghosts and Scholars, no. 16 (1993) *as* John Humphreys.

A Thin Ghost and Others by Montague Rhodes James. London: Edward Arnold, 1919.
A fine collection of antiquarian ghost fiction which has been slightly neglected by readers in favour of James' earlier two volumes.

The Book of the Queen's Doll's House Library edited by E. V. Lucas, with twenty-four plates, of which eight are in colour. London: Methuen & Co., 1924.
This includes the first appearance of James' story The Haunted Doll's House, *which had originally been written for inclusion in the miniature library of Queen Mary's doll's house. The book was published as part of a limited slipcased edition of 1,500 numbered copies, signed by King George V and Queen Mary, which also included* The Book of the Queen's Doll's House *edited by A.C. Benson and Sir Lawrence Weaver (1924).*

A Warning to the Curious and Other Ghost Stories by Montague Rhodes James. London: Edward Arnold &

Co., 1925.

An excellent supernatural collection, including the ghost story commissioned for the library of Queen Mary's doll's house, The Haunted Doll's House.

The Collected Ghost Stories of M. R. James. London: Edward Arnold & Co., 1931.

An omnibus collection of James' supernatural fiction, including some new material and an essay by James about his unsuccessful attempts at writing supernatural fiction, Stories I Have Tried to Write. *Several of the plot ideas he outlines in this essay were subsequently used by other authors writing their own ghost fiction or pastiches of James' work.*

Joseph Sheridan Le Fanu (1814-1873)

Joseph Sheridan Le Fanu, a descendant of the playwright, Richard Brinsley Sheridan, was born into an aristocratic Irish family at the height of the Gothic era. He was educated at Trinity College, Dublin, and following some success as a journalist, Le Fanu chose to test his entrepreneurial skills by becoming editor and proprietor of several Dublin publications; he combined the best of them to form the popular *Dublin Evening Mail.*

Le Fanu continued his successful literary career through the editorship of *Dublin University Magazine* between 1869 and 1872, and it was here that several of his supernatural and mystery stories first appeared. He is now regarded as one of the greatest exponents of the Victorian ghost story.

Le Fanu, who married in 1844, was devastated by the death of his wife in 1858 and in spite of his literary ventures spent much of the rest of his life as a semi-recluse. Plagued by bad dreams, Le Fanu's final years were made worse by mental stress and physical ill health. It was speculated that the heart attack that eventually ended his troubled life was brought on by one of his more vivid nightmares.

His first supernatural work, *The Ghost and the Bone Setter*, was published in 1838 and was highly influential in making a successful transition from the Gothic school to a more realistic and modern style of supernatural writing.

A perfectionist, he frequently rewrote his stories, sometimes after publication, and several were later reprinted under different titles.

Le Fanu was one of the first writers to introduce supernatural horror into the everyday world, dispassionately relating the psychological effects on his characters of ghostly events.

His treatment of themes such as vampirism and occult investigation became important influences on the genre, inspiring many other celebrated writers, including Bram Stoker, E.F. Benson and most notably, M.R. James. James was influenced by and championed Le Fanu's work, collecting several of the writer's rarest short stories in *Madam Crowl's Ghost* (1923).

Le Fanu's interest in mysticism and Irish folklore is clearly reflected in his work and his ghost stories about

Irish folk traditions are among his most successful. Le Fanu's best tales are notable for their originality and carefully measured development of atmosphere and tension. Many have an unusual dreamlike quality, which may possibly reflect their origins in Le Fanu's terrible nightmares.

In addition to his supernatural stories, Le Fanu developed a considerable reputation for his works of mystery and suspense, including his most famous work, *Uncle Silas* (1864).

Le Fanu's comprehensive mastery of the macabre has led many to compare his work to that of his American contemporary, Edgar Allen Poe.

Selected bibliography

Ghost Stories and Tales of Mystery with Illustrations by 'Phiz'. Dublin: James McGlashan; London and Liverpool: William S. Orr and Co., 1851.
An anonymously published early collection of Le Fanu's macabre fiction. A rare and much sought after volume.

In a Glass Darkly by J. Sheridan Le Fanu, in Three Volumes. London: R. Bentley & Son, 1872.
A truly classic collection of supernatural and mystery tales, including the seminal vampire novella Carmilla *and a masterpiece of psychological horror,* Green Tea. *The Familiar had been published previously as* The Watcher.

Madam Crowl's Ghost and Other Tales of Mystery by Joseph Sheridan Le Fanu; Collected and Edited by M.R. James. London: G. Bell and Sons Ltd., 1923.
An interesting collection of Le Fanu's supernatural fiction

containing many previously uncollected tales rediscovered by the
great ghost story writer M.R. James (see separate entry in this
volume). This publication includes an introduction to Le Fanu's
work by James.

The House by the Church-Yard by J. Sheridan Le
Fanu, in Three Volumes. London: Tinsley Brothers,
1863.
An excellent macabre mystery novel, including several
supernatural scenes later reprinted as self-contained short stories.

Chronicles of Golden Friars, in Three Volumes by J.
Sheridan Le Fanu. London: Richard Bentley, 1871.
An excellent Victorian ghost novel. Several sections have been
republished as self-contained short stories, including The
Haunted Baronet *and* Madam Crowl's Ghost.

Arthur Llewellyn Jones Machen (1863-1947)

Arthur Machen was born in the Welsh town of
Caerleon as Arthur Llewellyn Jones; his father later
changed the family's name to his wife's more unusual
maiden name, Machen.

In 1880, while still in his teens, Machen first visited
London, the city which would provide the backdrop
for many of his fictional works. He later moved there
to work as a translator and writer. In spite of its mid-
Victorian grime, Machen came to regard London as a
magical place, and seems to have found it as
inspirational as the countryside and folklore of his
native Wales.

Much of Machen's early work, such as *The Chronicle of*

Clemendy (1888), was influenced by French authors, most importantly François Rabelais, the French Renaissance doctor, writer and scholar. Although of some period interest, Machen's early work is inferior to his later more mature writing, beginning with the controversial novella *The Great God Pan* (1894). This work is notable for its unusual blend of science fiction, fantasy and the supernatural and is a reflection of Machen's increasing interest in magic and mysticism. Machen later joined several occult societies, including the infamous Golden Dawn.

After an initial period of literary success in the 1890s, Machen's popularity dwindled and this, coupled with the death of his wife, led him to become a travelling actor. Until the end of his long life, Machen regularly supplemented his irregular writer's income by working at a range of other jobs, including translator, teacher and clerk. But he remained a writer at heart in spite of his varying literary fortunes, and returned to his first love whenever he could.

During a spell working as a journalist for the *London Evening News* Machen produced what would become his most famous work, *The Bowmen* (1914), a propagandist short story that inspired the Angels of Mons myth. Although the tale came to be regarded as a true account of a supernatural visitation, Machen was always at pains to deny its factual basis. While initially glad to reap the financial rewards generated by the original story and several follow up pieces, Machen later came to feel it overshadowed his other more serious writing.

He continued to produce journalism and supernatural fiction on a regular basis and eventually received a literary pension. This was supplemented by a support fund set up by a growing number of admirers around the world, particularly in the United States. In later life, Machen developed a cult following and influenced many other writers who admired his work, most notably H.P. Lovecraft, who frequently acknowledged his inspiration.

A confirmed irrationalist and natural mystic, Machen disliked the introduction into fiction of scientific rationalism or the philosophy of materialism, and regularly used his writing to explore the elements of mystery present in everyday life.

Like his literary contemporary, Algernon Blackwood, Machen's fiction is more concerned with elemental forces of nature, rather than traditional ghosts. However, unlike Blackwood's more ambiguous and amoral nature spirits, Machen's elementals are somewhat darker, waiting in the wilder areas of the country to regain control of the earth from mankind and taking a cruel revenge on anyone unfortunate enough to cross their path or foolish enough to invoke them.

A recurring theme is a return to the folk belief that the benign fairies of children's stories have a less pleasant side to their nature; he portrays them as ancient and malevolent beings intent on causing death and suffering to humanity.

The continuing survival of pagan ritual and worship,

both in urban and rural settings, also features strongly in many of Machen's tales. In these works, supernatural forces directly challenge complacent rationalist assumptions about the world, presenting an interesting juxtaposition of the mundane and the mysterious.

While his potboiler commercial fiction may be dismissed as slight, and his prose as sometimes purple, Machen's best work has a poetic and mystical quality which is unparalleled among writers in the supernatural genre.

Machen's classic collection *Tales of Horror and the Supernatural* (1949) assembles many of his best works in the genre.

Selected bibliography

The Angels of Mons. The Bowmen and Other Legends of the War by Arthur Machen, with an Introduction by the Author. London: Simpkin, Marshall, Hamilton, Kent & Co. Ltd., 1915.
A collection of short propagandist tales involving supernatural intervention in the events of the First World War, including the infamous The Bowmen, *the source of one of the most enduring myths of the War.*

The Children of the Pool and Other Stories by Arthur Machen. London: Hutchinson & Co. (Publishers) Ltd., 1936.
A haunting collection of poetic supernatural and fantasy stories. Typical of the mature Machen style.

The Great God Pan, and, The Inmost Light by Arthur Machen. London: John Lane; Boston: Roberts Bros.,

1894.

Two excellent novella-length supernatural works. Controversial at the time of publication for their pagan themes and mild sexual content.

The Three Impostors, or, The Transmutations by Arthur Machen. London: John Lane; Boston: Roberts Bros., 1895.
A series of linked supernatural and horror stories set within the framework of a novel about a sinister secret society. Includes some of Machen's most powerful evocations of supernatural mystery and horror. The work was reprinted in 1966 as The Black Crusade.

The Green Round by Arthur Machen. London: Ernest Benn Limited, 1933.
An interesting macabre novel about the supernatural persecution of a student of the occult by elemental forces.

Oliver Onions (1863-1961)

Oliver Onions was born in Bradford, Yorkshire. He later changed his name to George Oliver, but kept Oliver Onions as his pen name. He originally worked as a commercial artist before beginning his literary career with the publication of his first book in 1900, (*The Compleat Bachelor*)

Although the bulk of Onions' literary output is mainstream fiction, he also experimented with various forms of genre writing, including science fiction, crime and ghost stories. However, it is for his supernatural work that Onions is now best known, and he is regarded by many as one of the 20th century masters of the genre. But although his ghost stories were admired by such notable contemporaries as Algernon Blackwood, it is unlikely that Onions himself attached any special significance his work in the supernatural genre.

Most of Onions' ghost stories date from a relatively short period at the start of his literary career, and are often notable for their depth of psychological insight, elegant prose and sophisticated plots. Several tales, including his most famous, *The Beckoning Fair One*, from the seminal collection, *Widdershins* (1911), draw on Onions' knowledge of artistic life gained during his early career as an illustrator.

The Beckoning Fair One, regarded by many as one of the greatest supernatural tales written in the English language, has overshadowed his other work in the genre which some consider of equal, if not greater, importance. Indeed, much of Onions' supernatural fiction is of an extremely high standard and notable for its originality, subtlety and careful characterisation. *The Rope in the Rafters*, for example, is a complex and richly ambiguous psychological study of a man living with the physical and mental aftermath of his wartime experiences.

Onions' ghost fiction is traditional in form, but he concentrates more fully than his contemporaries on his characters' inner feelings and physical reactions when faced with the seemingly inexplicable. A common theme in his work is the gradual breakdown of a personality following the realisation that supernatural forces are not confined to haunted castles of the past but can flourish in the contemporary everyday world. Interestingly, Onions was a great pragmatist and did not believe in ghosts or occult agencies of any sort. It is therefore testament to his writing skills that he so convincingly conveys supernatural atmosphere and events.

It should be noted that promising titles such as *The Ghost* in the collection *Admiral Eddy* (1907), *Ghosts in Daylight* (1924) and even *The Collected Ghost Stories of Oliver Onions* (1935) do not guarantee supernatural content.

One can only hope that Onions' supernatural fiction will one day receive the revival it so richly deserves.

Selected bibliography

Widdershins by Oliver Onions. London: Martin Secker, 1911.
An excellent collection of some of the twentieth century's greatest ghost stories. The Rocker *is omitted from some reprint editions of the collection.* Io, *which reappears in* The Collected Ghost Stories of Oliver Onions *as* The Lost Thyrsus, *is in fact a fantasy tale.*

The Painted Face by Oliver Onions. London: William Heinemann Ltd., 1929.
An excellent collection of three long supernatural tales.

Violet Paget (1856-1935)
(Pseudonym: Vernon Lee)

Violet Paget was born in the French town of Boulogne

to a Welsh mother and a father descended from the French nobility. The family travelled around Europe for several years before settling in the Italian city of Florence.

Despite her British citizenship, Paget did not visit England until 1881 and never chose to settle there. Under the pseudonym of Vernon Lee she developed a considerable reputation as a cultural historian of her adopted country of Italy, first attracting critical attention with her work, *Studies in Eighteenth Century Italy* (1880).

From this point she wrote a steady stream of essays, criticism and fiction chiefly about the history, art and literature of post-medieval Italy. Her lush descriptions of Renaissance and baroque culture in Florence and Rome appealed greatly to members of the aesthetic movement and were well suited to the spirit of *fin-de-siècle* decadence fashionable during the 1890s.

Although Paget wrote relatively few supernatural short stories, their quality gained her the respect of several connoisseurs of the genre, including M.R. James and Montague Summers*.

Not only do Paget's works have a psychological depth and subtlety rarely found in the genre, they also benefit from her detailed knowledge of Italian history and are packed with fascinating background detail.

It is difficult to generalise about Paget's ghostly fiction since it is highly diverse in both theme and setting. However, common motifs include the enduring power of evil and the illusory nature of time. Her stories also benefit greatly from her judicious use of humour and skilful writing technique.

Several reprint collections of Paget's macabre stories have been published under a variety of titles, including: *Supernatural Tales* (1955), *The Virgin of the Seven Daggers* (1962) and *Ravenna and Her Ghosts (1962).*

*Montague Summers (1880-1948) was an eccentric figure who wrote on the Gothic fiction genre, as well as producing works about witches, werewolves and vampires.

Selected bibliography

Hauntings: Fantastic Stories by Vernon Lee. London: William Heinemann, 1890.
An excellent collection of supernatural tales. The volume contains the ghostly novella, A Phantom Lover, *here given the title,* Oke of Okehurst.

Pope Jacynth and Other Fantastic Tales by Vernon Lee. London: Grant Richards, 1904.
A superior collection of varied and original ghostly tales. The volume was later reprinted as a Corgi paperback under the title Ravenna and Her Ghosts (1962).

For Maurice: Five Unlikely Stories by Vernon Lee. London: John Lane, The Bodley Head Limited, 1927.
The author's final supernatural collection assembles tales from her early career and is of extremely high quality throughout. The book is dedicated to another occasional writer of weird tales, Maurice Baring. Winthrop's Adventure *has also appeared in supernatural fiction anthologies as* A Cultured Ghost.

A Phantom Lover: A Fantastic Story by Vernon Lee. Edinburgh and London: William Blackwood and Sons, 1886.

A well-written short supernatural novel of great subtlety and some ambiguity, displaying a fine control of ghostly atmosphere. The story was also included in E.F. Bleiler's 1971 collection, Five Victorian Ghost Novels.

Mrs J.H. Riddell (1832-1906)

(Pseudonyms include: Rainey Hawthorne; R.V. Sparling; F.G. Trafford)

Charlotte Cowen, later Mrs Riddell, was born in Carrickfergus, County Antrim, into a relatively wealthy Anglo-Irish family. However, her father died during her youth, following financial ruin and Cowen moved with her mother to London, turning to writing to earn a living.

Cowen's mother did not live to see her daughter's remarkable success as a novelist, which began with the publication of her first book, *Zuriel's Grandchild* (1856). Shortly after her mother's death, Cowen married Joseph Riddell, a businessman with a rather mercurial personality.

Riddell based her most successful novels on her husband's detailed knowledge of London business life and gained a considerable reputation as a popular quality writer during the mid-Victorian period. In addition to her novels, Riddell contributed works to numerous magazines and Christmas annuals. However, as these were written under several pseudonyms or published anonymously, a complete bibliography of her work is problematic. Riddell also became editor and co-proprietor of *St James' Magazine*.

It is likely that Riddell's reputation as a mainstream novelist would have been greater if commercial pressures had not compelled her to increasingly sensationalise her fiction to satisfy her public.

In later life, as Riddell's popularity began to wane, she was further burdened by debts left by her husband following his death which she felt compelled to repay as a matter of honour. She eventually achieved this, but was then struck down by the illness which led to her death in 1906.

Riddell is acknowledged by connoisseurs as one of the greatest writers of supernatural fiction of the Victorian era and is particularly notable for creating ghost novels of sustained quality that remain of interest to this day. The author's ghost stories, which regularly draw on the folklore of her native Ireland, are particularly remarkable for their depth of characterisation and attention to background detail.

Unlike most of her contemporaries, Riddell managed to inject firm moral messages without resorting to sentimentality or artifice, her ghosts often acting as agents of retribution to redress past wrongs.

Together with Charles Dickens and Sheridan Le Fanu, Riddell helped to define the classic Victorian ghost story, but has not yet received the wider recognition she so thoroughly deserves.

Selected bibliography

Weird Stories by Mrs J.H. Riddell. London: J. Hogg, 1882.
A seminal collection of Victorian ghost stories containing the much anthologised The Open Door. *A reprint edition with an introduction by the ghost story anthologist Herbert Van Thal was published by Home & Van Thal in 1946.*

The Collected Ghost Stories of Mrs J.H. Riddell Selected and Introduced by E.F. Bleiler. New York: Dover Publications, Inc.; London: Constable and Company Ltd., c1977.
A useful collection of Riddell's short ghostly fiction, including the first UK book appearance of A Strange Christmas Game, *which has also been attributed to George A. Lawrence.*

Fairy Water: A Christmas Story by Mrs J.H. Riddell. London: George Routledge and Sons, 1873.
A high quality example of the Victorian ghost novel which has also been reprinted as The Haunted House at Latchford.

The Uninhabited House by Mrs J.H. Riddell. London: George Routledge and Sons, 1875.
Excellent supernatural novel, later included in E.F. Bleiler's Five Victorian Ghost Novels *(New York: Dover, 1971). The work was also reprinted as* The Haunted House at Latchford *in Bleiler's* Three Supernatural Novels of the Victorian Period *(New York: Dover, 1975).*

The Haunted River: A Christmas Story by Mrs J.H. Riddell. London: George Routledge and Sons, 1877.
A first class example of the Victorian ghost novel.

The Disappearance of Mr. Jeremiah Redworth by Mrs

J.H. Riddell. London: George Routledge and Sons, 1878.
An excellent supernatural novel. And the last of Riddell's highly successful series of contributions to Routledge's Christmas Annual.

Bram Stoker (1847-1912)

Born in Dublin, Bram Stoker attended the city's Trinity College to study law, but chose to join the civil service rather than pursue a legal career. In 1867, he became an unpaid drama critic for *The Dublin Mail* after submitting a review of the celebrated actor Henry Irving. The piece challenged the paper's negative appraisal and was well received.

Over the next decade, Stoker contributed a variety of articles and reviews to Irish magazines and newspapers, as well as trying his hand at fiction on several occasions. In 1877, he became manager of Henry Irving's theatre company, a position he was to hold for the rest of his life. Despite the demands of this work, Stoker still found time to produce a steady stream of fiction in addition to a biography of Irving. An early success was his collection of children's stories, *Under the Sunset* (1881).

The subjects of Stoker's stories for both adults and children are often macabre. His interest in the occult led him to investigate the subject in some depth and resulted in a short association with the infamous London magical society, the Golden Dawn. Stoker also befriended a Hungarian academic, Arminius Vambery, who provided him with much useful information on

Eastern European folklore and superstition; the result was Stoker's seminal work, the novel *Dracula* (1897)

Dracula proved an immediate popular success and quickly spawned many imitations. Although it was itself rather derivative of earlier vampire works, Stoker managed to renew interest in his subject matter by setting key scenes of the fragmentary narrative in contemporary England.

The combination of supernatural adventure, the exotic and the everyday proved irresistible to readers tired of traditional Victorian haunted house tales. While other sensational novels of the period, such as Richard Marsh's *The Beetle* (1897), rivalled it in popularity in the short term, *Dracula* has outlasted them all. In fact, the novel's influence quickly spread beyond the boundaries of supernatural fiction to achieve a cultural impact and influence few novels, either genre or mainstream, have ever approached.

Stoker's later works never matched the commercial or artistic success of *Dracula*. In comparison, they often seem shallow or confused, their subject matter dictated by contemporary preoccupations such as Balkan politics or Ancient Egypt.

Several novels were later extensively revised or abridged in unsuccessful attempts to increase their popularity. With the exception of a few imaginative short stories, *Dracula* is Stoker's only truly important legacy to supernatural literature. However, what a legacy!

Selected bibliography

Under the Sunset by Bram Stoker with Illustrations by W. Fitzgerald and W. V. Cockburn. London: Sampson Low, Marston, Searle, and Rivington, 1882.
Published in November 1881 and dedicated to Stoker's young son, this is an early children's collection of unusual fantasy and supernatural tales. Interesting and surprisingly macabre work both for the time and the intended audience.

Shades of Dracula: Bram Stoker's Uncollected Stories Edited by Peter Haining. London: William Kimber, 1982.
An interesting collection of rare stories and articles by Stoker and others. Most interesting is Vampires in New England *a short article from the* New York World *which Stoker had preserved in his notes and may have helped to inspire* Dracula.

Dracula by Bram Stoker. Westminster: Archibald Constable and Company, 1897.
Easily the most influential supernatural novel ever written and the origin of an entire vampire industry. Although filmed and adapted many times for stage and radio, no performance has yet managed to truly capture the atmosphere and originality of the novel itself. Numerous sections of the novel have over the years been extracted for inclusion in supernatural fiction anthologies appearing under such titles as Count Dracula, The Death of Dracula, Three Young Ladies, The Undead *and* The Vampire.

The Lair of the White Worm by Bram Stoker. London: William Rider and Son, Limited, 1911.
Arguably Stoker's best supernatural novel after Dracula. *Imaginative but poorly constructed. Published in America in 1966 as* Garden of Evil.

H.R. Wakefield (1888-1965)

Herbert Russell Wakefield was born in Elham, Kent, the son of an Anglican Vicar who later became the Bishop of Birmingham. Educated at Marlborough College and Oxford University, Wakefield's first job in 1911 was as Secretary to the press baron, Lord Northcliffe. This position gave Wakefield his first chance to write professionally and he began to contribute short pieces to Northcliffe's papers. When war broke out in 1914, Wakefield joined the Royal Scots Fusiliers serving in both France and Macedonia.

After the war, he returned to the world of literature, this time as a publisher. However, it was not until 1928 that he produced his first books, a light novel *Gallimaufry* and a highly regarded collection of ghost stories, *They Return at Evening*. The success of the latter led Wakefield to produce a follow-up a year later to yet further acclaim and suggestions that he might surpass even M.R. James as master of the English ghost story.

Wakefield began writing full time in 1930 and published several further ghost story collections as well as fiction and non-fiction works on crime. Wakefield's popularity waned after the Second World War as his rather refined and genteel writing style began to look increasingly anachronistic. He did, however, continue to publish stories in American pulp magazines throughout the 1950s, while pursuing a new career as a civil servant. A final collection of his 'pulp period' ghost stories was published in America only, but by this time Wakefield was becoming disillusioned with his ailing writing career.

A prolific author of short stories in several genres, the quality of Wakefield's numerous supernatural tales varies considerably. Most of his early stories are highly original, displaying a subtle manipulation of atmosphere combined with an urbane wit. The spirit of these stories is often close to that of M.R. James' although without the antiquarian detail. From the late 1930s, however, the tales increasingly seem to be written to a formula. Wakefield's attempts at modernising his restrained style with ever more horrific detail often make many of the later stories seem like crude imitations of their predecessors.

However, Wakefield did manage to recapture his old magic on a number of occasions, contributing a few first-rate items to magazines such as the celebrated *Weird Tales* as well as August Derleth's Arkham House anthologies. His final collection, *Strayers from Sheol* (1961), published in the United States only, includes several of these stories, although others remain uncollected.

Further material was incorporated in a limited new edition of the work published in Canada in 1999 by the Ash-Tree Press. The book, which forms part of a complete uniform edition of Wakefield's ghost stories, also includes a new introduction by Barbara Roden together with Wakefield's own suggested revisions to his tales.

Selected bibliography

They Return at Evening: A Book of Ghost Stories by H.R. Wakefield. London: Philip Allan & Co. Ltd., 1928.

An excellent collection of original and varied ghostly tales, including Wakefield's celebrated black magic story, He Cometh and He Passeth By. *The story* Professor Pownall's Oversight *has also appeared as* The Unseen Player. *The volume was reprinted by Ash-Tree Press (1995) with an introduction by Barbara Roden in a limited edition of 300 copies.*

Old Man's Beard: Fifteen Disturbing Tales by H.R. Wakefield. London: Geoffrey Bles, 1929.
A collection of high quality supernatural stories. It was issued in America under the title Others Who Returned *(1929). The volume was reprinted in 1996 by the Ash-Tree Press with a new introduction by Barbara Roden in a limited edition of 400 copies.*

Leading Literary Figures and the Ghost Story

Introduction

Charles Dickens' *A Christmas Carol* (1843), together with supernatural-themed seasonal editions of his magazines, helped create the traditional association of ghost stories with Christmas. Dickens was also able to call on other leading literary talent of the day when commissioning supernatural material, including Wilkie Collins and Elizabeth Gaskell; their more polished and sophisticated brand of ghost fiction gave further credibility to the genre as a potentially serious branch of mainstream literature, helping to usher in the golden age of the Victorian ghost story.

The challenges of writing successfully in the genre – a notoriously difficult one to master – combined with the potential scope for artistic expression would prove irresistible to many leading mainstream authors. From the late nineteenth to the early twentieth century, numerous giants of English literature would be attracted to the ghost story form.

An outstanding example is Henry James' *The Turn of the Screw*, a tale he referred to as his 'potboiler'. Subtle, ambiguous and deeply disturbing, this small masterpiece takes its place among the very best examples of the genre.

D.H. Lawrence and Oscar Wilde also made a unique contribution the genre, the former with among other tales, his much anthologised, *The Rocking Horse Winner,* and the latter with perhaps the most humorous ghost story ever written, *The Canterville Ghost,* as well as the enduringly popular supernatural tale, *The Picture of Dorian Gray,* Wilde's only published novel.

Also of particular interest are Thomas Hardy, whose ghost and Gothic fiction ranks among the best ever written, and Elizabeth Bowen, whose exceptionally sophisticated contribution to the genre is widely admired.

Other iconic writers who chose to write in the genre, sometimes with varying degrees of success, include Agatha Christie, E.M. Forster, L.P. Harley, H.G. Wells, Sir Walter Scott, and Robert Graves. Their contributions enrich the genre immeasurably.

DB

J.M. Barrie (1860-1937)

Born in Kirriemuir, Scotland, and educated at Dumfries Academy and Edinburgh University, James Matthew Barrie began his working life as a journalist. His first literary success came with a series of novels and short stories set in Thrums an imaginary Scottish town loosely based on Kirriemuir.

The critical acclaim for Barrie's stage adaptation of his successful novel, *The Little Minister* (1891), led him to concentrate more on drama, and a stream of successful works for the theatre followed. These included, *The Admirable Crichton* (1902), and *Peter Pan* (1904) which have now eclipsed the rest of his work.

Much of Barrie's writing reflects his lifelong interest in the ghostly and the fantastic, but he wrote few purely supernatural works and these were inferior in quality to his more mainstream writing. Towards the end of his life, Barrie's secretary, the prominent ghost story anthologist, Cynthia Asquith, helped to rekindle his interest in supernatural fiction. However, Barrie's last major work in the genre, a ghost novel, *Farewell Miss Julie Logan* (1931), was severely compromised by over-sentimentality and heavy use of Scots dialect.

Barrie's contribution to English literature was acknowledged when he became a baronet in 1913.

Selected bibliography

My Lady Nicotine by J.M. Barrie. London: Hodder and Stoughton, 1890.
A curious anthology of stories devoted to the pleasures of smoking a particular brand of tobacco. Includes a rarely published supernatural tale by Barrie, The Ghost of Christmas Eve.

The Black Cap: New Stories of Murder & Mystery Compiled by Cynthia Asquith. London: Hutchinson & Co. (Publishers), 1927.
This includes Barrie's ghost drama, Shall We Join the Ladies?

Portrait of Barrie by Cynthia Asquith. London: James Barrie, 1954.
Among the many memories of her time as Barrie's secretary, Asquith reveals how the onset of writer's cramp forced Barrie to write for a time with his left hand, which he claimed brought out

the sinister in him. Shall We Join the Ladies? *was apparently a product of his 'left hand period'.*

Arnold Bennett (1867-1931)

Arnold Bennett was born in North Staffordshire, the Potteries area that provides the setting for many of his best novels. He initially trained with his family's law firm before pursuing a career in journalism. Bennett took some time to develop as a fiction writer and later believed most of his early work was too commercial and below the standard of his mature output. Literary success finally came with the publication of novels such as *Anna of the Five Towns* (1902) and *Clayhanger* (1910) together with many other effective works of criticism, drama and short fiction.

He wrote a small number of supernatural and mystery tales, although these are not generally regarded as his most successful works. His novels, *The Ghost* (1907) and *The Glimpse* (1909), use the supernatural as a backdrop for what are basically morality tales. A sense of moral confusion coupled with a dose of dated Victorian melodrama spoil these otherwise well-written works.

Selected bibliography

The Ghost: A Fantasia on Modern Themes by Arnold Bennett. London: Chatto & Windus, 1907.
Originally published in periodical form as For Love and Life *in the 1890s. Bennett took unsuccessful legal action in an attempt to prevent the work's publication in book form since he believed it to be of such poor quality. An extract of the work has*

appeared in supernatural fiction anthologies under the title, The Ghost of Lord Clarenceux.

The Glimpse: An Adventure of the Soul by Arnold Bennett. London: Chapman & Hall Ltd., 1909.
A borderline supernatural novel about a man's experience of the afterlife, including evocative and original descriptions of Hell. Basically a psychological study in selfishness. A well-written if morally confused work.

Elizabeth Bowen (1899-1973)

Elizabeth Dorothea Cole Bowen was born in Dublin, but her father's ill health meant she spent much of her childhood with various relatives in England. The recurrent themes of loneliness and the disintegration of family bonds found in much of her work doubtless had their roots in this unhappy period.

Bowen achieved her first literary success as a writer of short stories, publishing the collection, *Encounters*, in 1923. A novel, *The Hotel*, followed in 1927, and she also worked as an essayist and biographer.

However, it was Bowen's fiction that contributed most to her growing reputation, its fine craftsmanship being coupled with a rare emotional depth and sensitivity, as in the successful novels, *The Death of the Heart* (1938) and *The Heat of the Day* (1949).

While Bowen did not believe the novel an appropriate literary form for the exploration of supernatural themes, her writing often implies the unreality of ordinary experience. However, she did successfully tackle the subject in several short stories which are widely considered important contributions to the genre.

An interesting feature of some of Bowen's tales is the combination of folk motifs and elements of traditional ghost fiction within a contemporary urban setting. The author's subtle treatment of the nature of time and human fear probably reflects her experiences during the London Blitz as much as her disrupted childhood.

Bowen's interest in the ghost story form is reflected both in the preface to her own short story collections and in her introduction to Cynthia Asquith's anthology, *The Second Ghost Book* (1952).

Bowen wrote a relatively small number of ghost stories, but they were of such a high standard that she is widely regarded as one of the genre's most sophisticated and mature writers.

Selected bibliography

The Demon Lover and Other Stories by Elizabeth Bowen. London: Jonathan Cape, 1945.
A general collection containing much supernatural material heavily influenced by Bowen's wartime experiences. Published in America under the title Ivy Gripped the Steps.

A Day in the Dark and Other Stories by Elizabeth Bowen. London: Jonathan Cape, c1965.
A collection of Bowen's best short stories containing an interesting preface by the author commenting on the use of supernatural themes in her work.

John Buchan (1875-1940)

Best known for his classic adventure tale, *The Thirty Nine Steps* (1915), John Buchan successfully combined a varied career in public service with a prodigious literary output.

Educated at Glasgow University, he trained as a solicitor before developing a number of commercial interests related to writing and journalism. He became part-owner of the publishers Thomas Nelson and later a director of the Reuters news agency. Buchan was elected to Parliament in 1927 and began a highly successful political career. He was given the title, 1st Baron Tweedsmuir in 1935 on his appointment as Governor General of Canada, a post he held until his death in 1940.

Although mainly a writer of adventure stories, Buchan experimented with several genres, including historical, ghost and science fiction. Many of his novels and short stories have supernatural or fantasy motifs, although these are usually incidental to the main plot. Common features of Buchan's supernatural work include the use of folklore and legend, often from his native Scotland, and a fascination with the nature of time. It has been suggested that his novel, *Sick Heart River* (1941), is a borderline supernatural work, but its themes are more metaphysical than macabre or ghostly.

Selected bibliography

The Watcher by the Threshold, and Other Tales by John Buchan. Edinburgh and London: William Blackwood and Sons, 1902.

A collection of good quality supernatural, fantasy and horror tales which also includes the popular mainstream story Fountainblue. The Far Islands *is a supernatural fantasy which shares some features with a traditional fairy tale.*

The Runagates Club by John Buchan. London: Hodder and Stoughton Limited, 1928.
A superior short story collection, including several supernatural tales, one featuring the first appearance of Buchan's recurring character, Richard Hannay. In Dr Lartius: Mr Palliser-Yeates's Story, *the theme of spirit communication is used but later rationalised.*

The Best Supernatural Stories of John Buchan Selected & Introduced by Peter Haining. London: Robert Hale, 1991.
A useful single volume collection of Buchan's most important supernatural fiction containing the first hardcover appearances of several tales. The Death Notice *is an extract from his novel* The Gap in the Curtain (1932). Basilissa *is an early version of a plot Buchan used for the novel,* The Dancing Floor *(1926).*

The Gap in the Curtain by John Buchan. London: Hodder and Stoughton, 1932.
A borderline supernatural novel concerning predestination and the nature of free will. The work was later republished in paperback as part of the Dennis Wheatley Library of the Occult *series.*

Agatha Christie (1890-1976)

Agatha Christie was born in Torquay, Devon, to an American father and English mother. She wrote her first novel, *The Mysterious Affair at Styles* (1930), while working in a Red Cross Hospital during the First World War: detective fiction would never be quite the same again.

Christie's interest in writing as a career was encouraged by a family friend and neighbour, the author Eden Phillpotts (1862-1960), and during her long career, Christie achieved a level of success in the crime fiction genre unknown since the days of the great Arthur Conan Doyle. A worldwide phenomenon, her works were translated into over one hundred languages. Even today it is rare for a month to pass without the broadcast of at least one of her plays, novels or short stories. Christie was awarded a CBE in 1951 for her contribution to English literature and was made a Dame Commander of the British Empire in 1971.

Before settling down to chronicle the exploits of characters such as Miss Marple and Hercule Poirot, Christie experimented with supernatural fiction in an early collection, *The Hound of Death and Other Stories* (1933).

The themes of justice and retribution found in her early writing were also explored in her later detective works. An attempt at fusing the ghost and crime genres through the character of a supernatural detective, Harley Quin, was not a great success, although Christie returned to the character several times during her writing career. Her late novel, *By the Pricking of my Thumb* (1968), features some black magic as background material.

Selected bibliography

The Mysterious Mr Quin by Agatha Christie. London: W. Collins Sons & Co. Ltd., c1930.
A strange hybrid work in which crimes are solved via the intervention of Harley Quin, an ambiguous supernatural entity. Quin acts via a human intermediary and seems to be a personification of the spirit of justice.

The Hound of Death and Other Stories by Agatha Christie. London: Odhams Press Limited, c1933.
Often trawled by anthologists, this collection of well-written tales in both the detective and ghost genres is lacking in originality although the supernatural tales are generally well handled. The main character in The Strange Case of Sir Andrew Carmichael *actually turns out to be called Arthur and in subsequent publications the story title is sometimes amended to correct this inconsistency. The collection is now chiefly remembered for the crime story,* A Witness for the Prosecution, *later successfully filmed.*

Miss Marple's Final Cases and Two Other Stories by Agatha Christie. London: Collins, 1979.
One of the two non-Marple stories, In a Glass Darkly, *is a supernatural tale.*

Wilkie Collins (1824-1889)

William Wilkie Collins was born in London, the son of a successful artist. Although Collins studied for the Bar, he never joined the legal profession, preferring to concentrate on a writing career. However, his first novel, *Antonina* (1850), received poor reviews and proved to be his last attempt at historical fiction.

Collins developed a close professional relationship with fellow author, Charles Dickens, eventually becoming editor of Dickens' *Household Words* magazine. The two men also collaborated on several stories but, as is common with such works, these were not as artistically successful as their individual output.

Collins gradually developed a reputation for well-crafted and highly ingenious mystery novels of which *The Moonstone* (1868) and *The Woman in White* (1860) are the best known today. The structure and style of these sophisticated works laid many of the foundations for the crime and thriller fiction genres.

While Collins' greatest strength is his ability to construct imaginative and well-paced plots, his works are also notable for their fine characterisation and attention to background detail. His suspense novels sometimes incorporate supernatural features and in common with many contributors to Dickens' magazines, he also wrote a number of short ghost stories which share the fine qualities of his mystery novels.

One feature common to Collins' crime and supernatural fiction is a strong sense of outrage at injustice. His detectives correct this moral imbalance in his novels while his ghosts act as catalysts for retribution in his supernatural tales. A further similarity is the exploration of individual reactions to the emotion of fear, whether induced by supernatural dread or sheer physical horror.

Throughout his life, Collins suffered periodic bouts of

ill health and in common with many contemporaries, including Queen Victoria, this led to an increasing dependence on the opium derivative, laudanum. His later work suffered because of this addiction and his final stories are of a considerably lower standard than his novels of the 1860s.

Nevertheless, there is still much for the supernatural fiction enthusiast to discover among Collins' early work. While a few of his tales have been regularly anthologised, excellent novels such as *Armadale* (1866) have been largely passed over in favour of his better-known works.

Selected bibliography

The Queen of Hearts by Wilkie Collins, in Three Volumes. London: Hurst and Blackett Publishers, Successors to Henry Colburn, 1859.
A general collection of linked stories, two of which have supernatural features: Brother Morgan's Story of the Dream-Woman *is a longer version of* The Ostler *which appeared in the 1855 Christmas number of* Household Words. *The story has been frequently reprinted as* The Dream Woman *or* Alicia Warlock. Brother Griffith's Story of Mad Monkton *originally appeared in* Fraser's Magazine *as* The Monktons of Wincot Abbey *and is usually anthologised as* Mad Monkton.

Armadale by Wilkie Collins with Twenty Illustrations by George H. Thomas in two volumes. London: Smith, Elder & Co., 1866.
An excellent mystery novel with strong supernatural features. Sophisticated and intricately constructed.

The Best Supernatural Stories of Wilkie Collins
Selected and Introduced by Peter Haining. London:
Robert Hale, 1990.
*A good selection of Collins' macabre work which also includes
some rare material such as* The Ostler, *the original version of
Collins' celebrated story,* The Dream Woman. The Dead
Hand *consists of chapter two of Collins' collaborative work with
Charles Dickens,* The Lazy Tour of Two Idle
Apprentices. John Jago's Ghost *is a crime story that
rationalises seemingly supernatural events.*

Walter de la Mare (1873-1956)

Walter de la Mare was born at Charlton in Kent and
educated at St Paul's School in London. He
contributed several short stories to magazines in the
late 1890s while working for an oil company, but
recognition of his talents did not come until the
publication of a volume of poems, *Songs of Childhood,* in
1902. The award of a civil pension in 1906 finally
allowed de la Mare to concentrate solely on his writing
and from this time he produced a steady and varied
stream of essays, poetry and fiction for adults and
children.

Compiling a definitive list of de la Mare's work is
complicated by several factors. In common with many
other authors, much of his work first appeared in
periodicals with some early pieces under pseudonyms.
More unusually, however, de la Mare's desire for
perfection often led him to revise works quite
substantially over time, with new editions of novels
such as *The Return* (1910) appearing throughout his life.
The author's short stories were also repackaged in a

variety of collections, regularly combining new and previously published material. In addition, many works were originally produced in limited editions with specially commissioned illustrations. His post as an executive at the publisher Faber and Faber doubtless assisted in these bibliographic variations.

Although de la Mare's first supernatural tale, *Kismet*, was published in magazine form in 1895, he did not write regularly in the genre until the 1920s. A fascination with the mysterious and the magical permeates much of de la Mare's work.

His children's stories are colourful fantasy tales of great vigour with a clear moral stance, while his adult fiction shares with his poetry an ambiguous dreamlike quality coupled with a subtle and lyrical beauty. His exploration of the relationships between the everyday world, the magical and the macabre was highly original and made a significant contribution to the supernatural genre.

Selected bibliography

The Return by Walter de la Mare. London: Edward Arnold, 1910.
A well-written and subtle metaphysical novel about evil possession. The story is written in a slightly different style from de la Mare's other macabre work. Revised editions of the novel were published in 1922 (London: W. Collins Sons & Co. Ltd) and 1945 (London: Faber and Faber).

The Riddle and Other Stories by Walter de la Mare. London: Selwyn & Blount Limited, 1923.
A general collection, including one of de la Mare's best-known

supernatural short stories, Seaton's Aunt. *This story was reprinted in London by Faber & Gwyer in 1927 with a wood-engraving on the front cover by Blair Hughes-Stanton.*

The Connoisseur and Other Stories by Walter de la Mare. London: W. Collins Sons & Co. Ltd., 1926.
A mainstream collection which includes de la Mare's best-known and most effective ghost story, All Hallows. *The story,* Mr Kemp, *is a rather ambiguous horror tale which has sometimes been included in supernatural fiction anthologies.*

They Walk Again: An Anthology of Ghost Stories chosen by Colin de La Mare with an introduction by Walter de la Mare. London: Faber & Faber Limited, 1931.
A collection of ghost stories assembled by de la Mare's son that includes an interesting introduction by Walter de la Mare as well as his popular story, All Hallows.

The Wind Blows Over by Walter de la Mare. London: Faber and Faber Limited, 1936.
A wonderful collection of de la Mare's supernatural and fantasy tales. A limited edition of seventy-five numbered copies on handmade paper was issued later in the same month.

Charles Dickens (1812-1870)

Charles Dickens was born in the naval town of Portsmouth where his father worked in the Royal Navy's pay department. His education was disrupted by his family's moves to Chatham, Kent, and eventually London, where financial problems led to his father being sent to debtor's prison.

Dickens first worked as an articled clerk in a lawyer's office before joining the prestigious *Morning Chronicle* as a reporter. The series of magazine articles he wrote during this early period were later collected as *Sketches by Boz* (1836). It was on the strength of this work that Dickens was commissioned to write *The Posthumous Papers of the Pickwick Club*, which appeared in serial form from 1837. In the same year, he became editor of the periodical *Bentley's Miscellany*. *The Pickwick Papers* established Dickens' reputation and he went on to produce a string of successful novels, including *Nicholas Nickleby* (1838), *Martin Chuzzlewit* (1844) and *Bleak House* (1853).

During his lifetime, Dickens was editor and proprietor of several successful magazines, including *Household Words* (1850-1859) and *All the Year Round* (1859-1870). In addition to his own work, these magazines frequently contained contributions from other notable authors of the period, including Mrs Gaskell and Wilkie Collins. Dickens was an amazingly prolific author, and the volume and quality of his output is all the more impressive considering the tight commercial deadlines he was forced to meet.

While aspects of Dickens' work may now seem sentimental and melodramatic, he was completely in tune with contemporary public taste and enormously popular both in Britain and America. In some respects, he acted as the conscience of Victorian society, his sympathetic portrayals of poverty and hardship owing much to his own childhood experiences. A master storyteller, Dickens was also a gifted reader of his own work, and travelled widely giving dramatic readings to appreciative audiences. A combination of overwork and extensive travelling almost certainly contributed to Dickens' early death in 1870.

As a child, Dickens had been introduced to the supernatural through the tales of his nurse maid, Mary Weller. He was also an avid reader of the popular 'penny dreadfuls' which regularly chronicled horrific and ghostly events. Dickens' interest in the macabre continued throughout his life and he incorporated aspects of the supernatural and grotesque into several of his mainstream novels, including *Nicholas Nickleby, The Pickwick Papers,* and in particular, *Bleak House,* which includes a description of spontaneous human combustion.

The publication of one of Dickens' most enduringly popular works, *A Christmas Carol* (1843), began the association of Christmas with supernatural tales, and he encouraged other authors to write ghost stories for the Christmas numbers of his magazines; this cemented the link between the festive and the ghostly in popular culture – a tradition which continues to the present.

In addition to the more famous *A Christmas Carol,* Dickens also produced a similar moralistic dream fantasy, *The Chimes* (1844), sections of which have occasionally appeared in anthologies of supernatural or fantasy fiction.

Dickens' ghost fiction ranges from the humorous to the horrific and, in common with much of his other work, frequently delivers a moral message. While he produced relatively few supernatural stories, Dickens' encouragement of serious authors to attempt ghostly fiction was a crucial factor in transforming the ghost story from a pulp genre to a respectable literary form, laying the foundations for the golden age of Victorian supernatural writing.

Selected bibliography

Charles Dickens' Christmas Ghost Stories Selected and Introduced by Peter Haining. London: Robert Hale, 1992.

An excellent collection of Dickens' supernatural tales, most of which were published in the Christmas editions of All the Year Round *and* Household Words magazines. *The anthology includes Dickens' essay on spiritualism,* Ghosts and Ghost-Seers *together with his satire on the same subject,* The Rapping Spirits.

The Complete Ghost Stories of Charles Dickens Edited and Introduced by Peter Haining. London: Michael Joseph, 1982.

The most comprehensive collection of Dickens' supernatural stories together with a detailed critical introduction by the ghost story anthologist Peter Haining. The work includes two anonymous items: Four Ghost Stories *and* The Portrait Painter's Story, *from* All the Year Round *which Haining believes are by Dickens.*

Extracts from Household Words, relating to Mr. C. Dickens' visit to Lancaster; with extracts from the Official Illustrated Guide of the Lancaster & Carlisle, Caledonian and Edinburgh & Glasgow Railways; also, description of the torch-light procession in Lancaster, on the marriage of H.R.H. the Prince of Wales, March

10th 1863. Lancaster: printed by G.C. Clark, Gazette Office, 1866.

A collaboration with Wilkie Collins (see separate entry on this author). Included in chapter four is a self-contained ghost story which has been reprinted under the title The Ghost and the Bridal Chamber.

The Posthumous Papers of the Pickwick Club by Charles Dickens with Forty-Three Illustrations by R. Seymour and Phiz. London: Chapman & Hall, 1837.

Humorous work that established Dickens' literary reputation. It includes several self-contained supernatural tales: The Lawyer and the Ghost, The Queer Chair, The Ghosts of the Mail, A Madman's Manuscript *and* The Story of the Goblins Who Stole a Sexton.

The Life and Adventures of Nicholas Nickleby. London: Chapman & Hall, 1839.

A mainstream novel that includes a self-contained supernatural tale, Baron Koëldwethout's Apparition.

A Christmas Carol in Prose: Being a Ghost-Story of Christmas by Charles Dickens with Illustrations by John Leech. London: Chapman & Hall, 1843.

One of Dickens' most successful works and certainly the most popular ghost story ever written. A section of the work has also been anthologised under the titles, Marley's Ghost *and* Old Marley's Ghost.

Sir Arthur Conan Doyle (1859-1930)

Arthur Conan Doyle was born in Edinburgh where he trained and practised as a doctor before becoming a professional author. Doyle first established his reputation as a writer of sensational adventure and mystery stories for several popular magazines, including *Temple Bar* and *The Strand* and it was in the 1887 edition of *Beeton's Christmas Annual* that the author's most famous character, Sherlock Holmes, first appeared: Doyle's life and detective fiction would never be the same again.

Nevertheless, despite the success of the Holmes stories, Doyle continued to write in a variety of genres. He was particularly attracted to the historical novel, believing that his historical works, for example, *Sir Nigel* (1906), were his greatest literary achievement.

Sometimes a controversial figure, Doyle championed several campaigns relating to miscarriages of justice, achieving some notable successes, including reform of the divorce law and the release of the falsely imprisoned Oscar Slater. He was knighted in 1902 for services during the Boer War.

In spite of his scientific training, Doyle was fascinated by the mysterious and supernatural and nearly a third of his short stories deal with various aspects of the uncanny. While early tales are sensationalist, incorporating the macabre simply for heightened dramatic effect, Doyle's later supernatural fiction reflects his conversion during the First World War to the spiritualist cause.

Even some of the Holmes stories, most notably *The Hound of the Baskervilles* (1902), contain supernatural touches, although these are always eventually given a rational explanation. While Doyle never used Holmes in a truly supernatural plot, he did utilise another popular character, the scientist Professor Challenger, in a spiritualist novel, *The Land of Mist* (1926).

Doyle spent much of his later life investigating occult phenomena and produced several non-fiction works on the subject. He also provided inspiration to writers of supernatural tales and appeared in the title story of Leslie Halliwell's collection, *The Ghost of Sherlock Holmes* (1984).

Doyle's supernatural short stories vary significantly in quality from low-grade sensationalist pulp fiction to sophisticated stories examining human reactions to the unknown. Most tales, however, display the storytelling skills that made Doyle one of the most popular writers of his era, often combining original plot ideas with exotic background material. One example is *The Ring of Thoth* (1890), occasionally anthologised in supernatural fiction collections as *The Mummy*, a tale that blended the popular craze for Ancient Egypt with magic and science fiction themes.

Although they never achieved the popularity of his detective works, Doyle's supernatural tales are well worth exploring and provide an interesting counterpoint to the more extreme rationalism of the Holmes stories.

Selected bibliography

Round the Red Lamp: Being Facts and Fancies of Medical Life by A. Conan Doyle. London: Methuen & Co., 1894.
A collection of short stories drawing upon Doyle's medical

experiences, including one of his most popular supernatural tales, Lot No. 249.

Round the Fire Stories by Arthur Conan Doyle. London: Smith, Elder & Co., 1908.
One of Doyle's best short story collections, including miscellaneous adventure, mystery and macabre tales as well as several of his most anthologised ghost stories.

Tales of the Ring and the Camp by Arthur Conan Doyle. London: John Murray, 1922.
As the title suggests, a collection of stories about wrestling, boxing and army life. The work contains Doyle's most effective ghostly tale, The Bully of Brocas Court.

The Mystery of Cloomber by A. Conan Doyle. London: Ward and Downey, 1889.
A poor-quality and derivative occult thriller involving the revenge of an Indian cult upon the family of a man who murdered one of their members.

The Parasite by A. Conan Doyle. Westminster: A. Constable, 1894.
A short sensationalist novel exploring the perils of spiritualism, written before Doyle's conversion to the cause.

The Edge of the Unknown by Arthur Conan Doyle. London: John Murray, 1930.
Doyle's most significant work on the subject of spiritualism.

E.M. Forster (1879-1970)

Edward Morgan Forster is generally regarded as one of the greatest English novelists of his generation.

Educated at Cambridge University, Forster maintained a lifelong relationship with King's College. Literary success came in 1905 with his first novel *Where Angels Fear to Tread*, and his reputation grew steadily with the publication of *A Room with a View* (1908) and his masterpiece, *Howard's End* (1910).

Forster was a member of the Bloomsbury Group of writers, creating much of his fiction during the group's heyday, with six novels and two short story collections appearing in the first three decades of the twentieth century.

Following this particularly creative period, Forster devoted his considerable literary talents to works of literary criticism, biography and essays. A committed campaigner against literary censorship, his novel of homosexual love, *Maurice*, completed in 1914, remained unpublished until after his death in 1970.

Forster's importance to supernatural fiction lies with his two early short story collections which chiefly comprise fantasies exploring inter-relationships between the unusual or inexplicable and the mundane.

Several tales, although not traditional ghost stories, feature supernatural themes and it is interesting that such a pillar of the English literary establishment found the subject a valid and rewarding inspiration for artistic expression. It's possible that his interest in the subject may have been prompted by a fellow resident of his beloved King's College, M.R. James (featured in this volume), who was Provost during Forster's time as an undergraduate student.

Selected bibliography

The Celestial Omnibus and Other Stories by E.M. Forster. London: Sidgwick & Jackson Ltd., 1911.
A collection of fantasy and supernatural material of exceptional quality. While the title work has regularly appeared in supernatural fiction anthologies, few of the other tales have been reprinted.

The Story of the Siren by E.M. Forster. Richmond: Printed by Leonard & Virginia Woolf at The Hogarth Press, 1920.
A single supernatural short story published in a limited edition of 500 copies. The work later reappeared in Forster's collection, The Eternal Moment and Other Stories *(1928).*

The Eternal Moment and Other Stories by E.M. Forster. London: Sidgwick & Jackson Ltd., 1928.
A sophisticated collection of borderline supernatural tales focusing on the afterlife. The collection also contains Forster's much anthologised science fiction story, When the Machine Stops.

Mrs Gaskell (1810-1865)

Elizabeth Cleghorn Stevenson was born in London but following the early death of her mother was brought up in Knutsford, Cheshire, by an aunt. At the age of 21, she married William Gaskell, a Unitarian minister, and went to live with him in the industrial city of Manchester. Encouraged by her husband, Gaskell began to write, at first in collaboration with him and later on her own.

After several years of writing short magazine pieces, literary success came in 1848 with the publication of her novel *Mary Barton*. Charles Dickens was impressed by Gaskell's work, and invited her to contribute material to his popular magazine *Household Words*. Much of Gaskell's work, including the celebrated novel *Cranford* (1853), made its first appearance in the magazine. During this period, Gaskell became friends with the writer Charlotte Brontë and later wrote a classic biography of her fellow novelist.

Gaskell's supernatural fiction ranks among the best of the Victorian period, with several of her most famous tales, including, *The Old Nurse's Story* (1852) and *The Squire's Story* (1853), originally appearing in Christmas issues of *Household Words*. Gaskell's ghost tales are scattered throughout various periodicals and books of short stories and no single volume collection existed until 1978 when Michael Ashley produced *Mrs Gaskell's Tales of Mystery and Horror*.

Together with Dickens' work, Gaskell's ghost fiction helped consolidate the association of the supernatural tale with the Victorian Christmas. Gaskell claimed to have seen a ghost and her belief in their reality may have added an extra dimension to her macabre writing. However, the main reason for her success is the combination of superb narrative technique and skilled control of atmosphere.

An additional reason for the popularity of Gaskell's supernatural work during the Victorian period is its lack of moral ambiguity. While some modern readers might find this moralistic standpoint a little simplistic, there is no doubting the effectiveness of Gaskell's writing. Most of her ghost stories are as enjoyable today as when they first appeared.

Selected bibliography

Round the Sofa by the Author of 'Mary Barton', 'Life of Charlotte Brontë', &c. &c., Two Volumes. London: Sampson Low, Son & Co., 1859.
A series of linked stories told in Margaret Dawson's sitting room in Edinburgh. The work includes The Doom of the Griffiths *which was Gaskell's first ghost story and* The Poor Clare, *about the effects of a curse.*

Right at Last and Other Tales by the Author of 'Mary Barton', 'Life of Charlotte Brontë', 'Round the Sofa' &c. London: Sampson Low, Son & Co., 1860.
The first book appearance of Lois the Witch *which had appeared in periodical form in* All the Year Round *during the previous year. An illustrated edition of Gaskell's short witchcraft novel was published in 1960 in London by Methuen, with pictures by Faith Jaques.*

The Grey Woman and Other Tales by Mrs Gaskell. London: Smith Elder & Co., 1865.
A mainstream collection of stories containing the supernatural tale, Curious if True.

Robert Graves (1895-1985)

Although he later gained fame as a prose writer, Robert Graves was first acclaimed as one of the best war poets to emerge from a generation decimated on the Western Front. Graves went on to describe his war experiences in his autobiographical work, *Good-bye to All That* (1929).

Throughout his long life, Graves was fascinated by the subjects of mythology and religion, particularly those of the classical and Celtic worlds. He eventually came to believe that the life and work of the poet should be intimately linked to the religious and social life of his fellow citizens in a manner similar to that of the ancient Celtic bards.

Although Graves wrote extensively on his favourite subjects, works such as the *White Goddess* (1959) and *The Greek Myths* (1955) were overshadowed by the success of his bestselling novels on Imperial Rome, *I Claudius* (1934) and *Claudius the God and His Wife Messalina* (1934).

Supernatural subject matter was incorporated into several of Graves' fiction and non-fiction works, although often with a degree of ambiguity. While this qualification might concern a strictly 'purist' reader of supernatural fiction, Graves' stories are thought-provoking and highly polished works, offering an entertaining and original contribution to the genre.

Selected bibliography

The Shout by Robert Graves. London: Elkin Mathews & Marrot, 1929.
An interesting and original tale about aboriginal black magic which was later filmed starring Alan Bates in the lead role. The work was published in a limited edition of 530 numbered copies.

¡Catacrok!: Mostly Stories, Mostly Funny by Robert

Graves. London: Cassell & Co. Ltd., 1956.
A general collection that includes The White Horse, *a ghost story based on folk legends, and the witchcraft tale,* An Appointment for Candlemas.

Thomas Hardy (1840-1928)

Thomas Hardy was born in Higher Bockhampton, Dorset, the son of a local stonemason. After leaving school, he trained as an ecclesiastical architect, eventually moving to London to develop his career.

Hardy published his first short story in 1865 and his first novel, *Desperate Remedies*, in 1871. A succession of critically acclaimed and commercially successful works followed, including *Far from the Madding Crowd* (1874) and *The Return of the Native* (1878). It was in these early works that Hardy first began to examine the related subjects of fate and mortality, themes that became increasingly central to much of his poetry and prose.

Hardy's later novels were attacked for their bleak and uncompromising portrayal of rural life, and for the final period of his literary career he concentrated on writing poetry and occasional short stories.

A firm believer in the supernatural, Hardy claimed to have seen and spoken with a ghost, possibly that of his grandfather, one Christmas Eve. Following the established Victorian tradition, some of Hardy's ghost stories have Christmas settings, while several draw inspiration from the legends and folklore of his native Dorset.

Hardy's poetry and fiction often contain macabre motifs, with death and its portents featuring frequently, even in his more mainstream material. As a result, several of his tales have often been included in supernatural fiction anthologies despite having no real supernatural content. Among many examples of this type of work are, *Barbara of the House of Grebe* (1890), *What the Shepherd Saw* (1881) and most famously, *The Three Strangers* (1883).

Hardy rarely wrote tales in which the supernatural took centre stage, preferring to use it as background material for works exploring the nature of fate or evil.

The diverse, if sometimes peripheral, ways in which Hardy made use of macabre and supernatural subjects is particularly apparent in Peter Haining's collection, *The Supernatural Tales of Thomas Hardy* (1988).

Hardy's ghostly and Gothic fiction are acknowledged as among the most artistically satisfying ever produced and are valuable contributions to both the supernatural genre and English literature in general.

Selected bibliography

Wessex Tales: Strange, Lively, and Commonplace by Thomas Hardy, in Two Volumes. London and New York: Macmillan and Co., 1888.
A celebrated collection of rural short stories, including one of Hardy's most famous supernatural tales, The Withered Arm.

The Supernatural Tales of Thomas Hardy Edited by Peter Haining. London: W. Foulsham & Co. Ltd., c1988.

A miscellaneous collection of assorted short fiction and factual pieces dealing with supernatural, fantasy or horror subjects. In addition to his better known work, the volume includes several previously uncollected short stories together with some borderline pieces, including the macabre What the Shepherd Saw; *the Gothic* Barbara of the House of Grebe; *and fairy tale fantasies such as* The Romantic Adventures of a Milkmaid.

L.P. Hartley (1895-1972)

Leslie Poles Hartley was educated at Harrow and Balliol College, Oxford, before serving in the Norfolk Regiment throughout the First World War. The horrors Hartley experienced during this conflict probably provided the inspiration for the dark atmosphere of much of his later fiction.

His first short story collection, *Night Fears*, was published in 1924, swiftly followed by a short novel, *Simonetta Perkins* (1925). However, his literary reputation over the next two decades would be founded on his works of criticism rather than his fiction.

While the high quality of Hartley's criticism was acknowledged by writers and fellow critics alike, his skills as a fiction writer were not recognised until the publication of *The Shrimp and the Anemone* (1944), the first volume of his Eustace and Hilda trilogy. Hartley went on to win several literary prizes with two novels, *The Go-Between* (1953) and *The Hireling* (1957), both later adapted as successful films.

Much of Hartley's work has macabre overtones and the distinction between his supernatural and mainstream fiction is sometimes blurred. An example is the ghostly section of the novel, *Eustace and Hilda* (1947).

Throughout his career, Hartley contributed stories to Cynthia Asquith's ghost story anthologies and much of his best work first appeared in these collections. His finest supernatural work demonstrates an outstanding ability to create and sustain a ghostly atmosphere through subtle plot development and keen psychological insight. The tales are made all the more unique by Hartley's sophisticated blend of ambiguity, horror and humour.

August Derleth, the celebrated anthologist and founder of the American Arkham House publishing company, collected many of Hartley's supernatural writings in *The Travelling Grave and Other Stories* (1948). However, it should be noted that many of the tales in this collection are in the horror or crime genre and are not ghostly.

Selected bibliography

The Ghost Book: Sixteen New Stories of the Uncanny Compiled by Lady Cynthia Asquith. London: Hutchinson and Co. (Publishers) Ltd., 1926.
This contains one of Hartley's most celebrated and regularly anthologised ghost stories, A Visitor from Down Under.

The Children's Cargo: Lady Cynthia Asquith's Annual; Contributions by A.A. Milne, Hilaire Belloc, Algernon Blackwood, Walter De la Mare, Henry Williamson, Arthur Machen, 'Beachcomber', Denis Mackail, Rose

Fyleman, etc., etc. London: Eyre & Spottiswoode (Publishers) Ltd., 1930.
This includes Hartley's supernatural children's story, Conrad and the Dragon, *illustrated by Daphne Jerrold.*

The Killing Bottle by L.P. Hartley. London & New York: Putnam, 1932.
A collection containing much of Hartley's best supernatural material, the bulk of which was previously published in anthologies and periodicals.

The White Wand and Other Stories by L.P. Hartley. London: Hamish Hamilton, 1954.
A general collection, including three supernatural stories.

The Third Ghost Book Edited by Cynthia Asquith. London: James Barrie, 1955.
This includes an introduction by Hartley together with his regularly reprinted tale, Someone in the Lift.

Mrs Carteret Receives and Other Stories by L.P. Hartley. London: Hamish Hamilton, 1971.
A general collection containing three short supernatural tales.

Eustace and Hilda by L.P. Hartley. London: Putnam & Co. Ltd., 1947.
The final novel in Hartley's acclaimed trilogy includes a significant supernatural scene.

Henry James (1843-1916)

Henry James was born in New York, but raised and educated mainly in Europe, a continent he came to regard as his spiritual home. James returned to America in 1860 to study law at Harvard University but found literature more appealing than the legal profession and soon began to submit short stories to magazines in the hope of becoming a professional writer.

His first success came with the publication of *The Story of a Year* in the *Atlantic Monthly* in 1865 and this began a long association with the periodical. In 1869 James emigrated to England where he remained for the rest of his life, finally becoming a British citizen in 1915.

James' first novel, *Watch and Ward* was published in 1871 but it was not until *Roderick Hudson* (1875) that his work began to receive significant critical attention. The next decade was arguably the most artistically successful of James' career with major works, including *Daisy Miller* (1878), *Washington Square* (1880) and *Portrait of a Lady* (1881), appearing in rapid succession. Many of the author's novels explore the changing relationship between American and European society at a time when the power of the New World was beginning to eclipse that of the old.

James' work was less commercially successful during the 1890s, although by this time he had developed a considerable reputation amongst both writers and critics as a master prose stylist. After an ill-fated attempt at writing drama, success returned in 1897 with a novel, *The Awkward Age*. A year later, James produced what would come to be regarded by many as one of the greatest supernatural stories ever written: *The Turn of the Screw*.

James had already written several ghost stories during

his career and after a number of more conventional early tales developed a subtle and thought-provoking style of supernatural writing that was uniquely his. Several influences were important in James' 'interior' approach to the uncanny, but probably most significant were the theories of his brother, William James, the famous psychologist, who had made a detailed study of human reactions to religion and the supernatural.

The particular inspiration for *The Turn of the Screw* came from an anecdote related by Archbishop Benson, father of the three Benson brothers mentioned elsewhere in this volume. James reworked Benson's tale extensively, emphasising one of his favourite themes – possession of an individual by evil forces – and succeeded in creating a masterpiece which has fascinated and horrified readers since it was first published.

The story has been adapted for a variety of media, being filmed as *The Innocents* (1961) and turned into an opera by Benjamin Britten in 1954. Ironically, the work's reception seems to have surprised and puzzled James who regarded it as something of a potboiler. In 1997, Hilary Bailey wrote a sequel, *Miles and Flora*.

James continued to write occasionally in the ghost genre for the rest of his life, although he never again created a piece to rival the power of *The Turn of the Screw*.

An attempt to write a full-length supernatural novel foundered and the incomplete manuscript was published posthumously as *The Sense of the Past* (1917).

Although sometimes criticised for his perceived verbosity and overcomplicated literary style, James' reputation continued to grow in the years following his death and he is now regarded as one of the most significant figures of modern English literature.

The quality of James' supernatural writing assures him of equal stature among writers of the genre.

Selected bibliography

Stories Revived: in Three Volumes by Henry James. London: Macmillan and Co., 1885.
A general collection of short stories, including some supernatural tales such as The Romance of Certain Old Clothes *which are written in a more traditional style than James' later work.*

The Lesson of the Master: The Marriages, The Pupil, Brooksmith, The Solution, Sir Edmund Orme by Henry James. London and New York: Macmillan and Co., 1892.
A general collection, including one of James' most anthologised ghost stories, Sir Edmund Orme, *the first of his supernatural stories to be written from a psychological viewpoint.*

The Private Life: The Wheel of Time, Lord Beaupre, The Visits, Collaboration, Owen Wingrave by Henry James. London: James R. Osgood, McIlvaine & Co., 1893.
A general collection, including one of James' most subtle and interesting macabre stories, Owen Wingrave.

Embarrassments: The Figure in the Carpet, Glasses, The Next Time, The Way it Came by Henry James. London: William Heinemann, 1896.
A general collection, including an ambiguous but deftly handled ghost story, The Way it Came. *This work has also been reprinted as* The Friends of the Friends.

The Two Magics: The Turn of the Screw, Covering End by Henry James. London: William Heinemann, 1898.
Two novella-length tales, one of which is James' supernatural masterpiece The Turn of the Screw: *arguably the greatest psychological ghost story ever written.*

The Soft Side by Henry James. London: Methuen & Co., 1900.
An excellent mainstream short story collection containing some first-class ghostly tales. James at his very best.

The Better Sort by Henry James. London: Methuen & Co., 1903.
A general collection, including the psychological ghost story, The Beast in the Jungle, *a work considered by some to be James' greatest short story achievement.*

In After Days: Thoughts on the Future Life by W.D. Howells, Henry James, John Bigelow, Thomas Wentworth Higginson, Henry M. Alden, William Hanna Thomson, Guglielmo Ferrero, Julia Ward Howe, Elizabeth Stuart Phelps, with portraits. New York and London: Harper & Brothers Publishers, 1910.
The chapter by Henry James is entitled, Is There a Life After Death?

Rudyard Kipling (1865-1936)

Born in Bombay, Rudyard Kipling was sent to England at the age of five to be educated at the United Services College at Westward Ho, Devon. The publication of his first book of poems, *Schoolboy Lyrics* (1881), was financed by his parents. Kipling returned to India in 1882 to begin a journalistic career as sub-editor of the *Lahore Civil and Military Gazette*, and it was in this journal that the Indian tales which made up his earliest short story collections first appeared.

With a growing reputation, Kipling returned once again to England and published his first full-length work, *The Light that Failed* (1891). His fame then increased with the publication of his popular verse in the *National Observer*.

Kipling moved to America following his marriage in 1892, and during the four years he spent living in Vermont, he created two of his most enduring works, *The Jungle Book* (1894) and its sequel, *The Second Jungle Book* (1895).

Kipling returned to England to settle permanently in 1896 and enjoy the huge popularity his works had brought him. Further success with verse, such as *Recessional* (1897), and fiction, including the popular *Kim* (1901), resulted in Kipling becoming the first English writer to win the Nobel Prize for Literature in 1907.

Kipling's reputation began to decline after the First World War when his brand of imperialist adventure lost favour with a generation disillusioned by war, and his jingoistic reputation may still deter some potential readers.

Kipling's later work may be viewed as propagandist, but his early stories can be enjoyed today for their original plots, fine characterisation and exotic background detail.

The bulk of his supernatural tales date from this period and display Kipling's storytelling powers at their best. In addition to more conventional ghost tales, he excels at ambiguous or rationalised stories in which the nature of occult phenomena is examined from a variety of viewpoints.

The most notable examples are, *My Own True Ghost Story* from *The Phantom Rickshaw* (1888) and *The Haunted Subalterns* from the third edition of *Plain Tales from the Hills* (1896). In later years, while still capable of the occasional excellent tale such as *They* (1905), Kipling preferred to tackle more mainstream subjects and rarely returned to the macabre with any degree of conviction.

Selected bibliography

Plain Tales from the Hills by Rudyard Kipling. Calcutta: Thacker, Spink and Co.; London: W. Thacker and Co., 1888.
The first publication of Kipling's celebrated collection of Indian stories containing several magical and supernatural tales. The more widely available Macmillan edition of 1890 helped to assure Kipling's reputation as one of the most important writers of his generation.

The Phantom 'Rickshaw and Other Tales. Allahabad: A. H. Wheeler & Co.; London: Sampson Low Martson, Searle & Rivington, 1890.

This is the first UK appearance of Kipling's collection of original and entertaining tales reprinted from The Week's News *and originally published in 1888 in Allahabad, India. With the exception of* The Man Who Would be King *all the tales have supernatural features. A facsimile of the first edition was published in 1988 by the R. S. Surtees Society.*

Life's Handicap: Being Stories of Mine Own People by Rudyard Kipling. London: Macmillan and Co., 1891.

A general collection of stories set in India with several horror and supernatural items, including one of Kipling's great supernatural genre works, The Mark of the Beast.

Traffics and Discoveries by Rudyard Kipling. London: Macmillan and Co. Limited, 1904.

A general collection containing one of the earliest supernatural stories to feature a wireless, aptly named Wireless. *This volume also includes Kipling's most successful ghostly tale,* They.

D.H. Lawrence (1885-1930)

Born the son of a miner at Eastwood in Nottinghamshire, David Herbert Lawrence was to become one of the most revolutionary figures of 20th century English literature. Lawrence left Nottingham High School at fifteen to work as a clerk and later trained as a teacher.

However, poor health forced him to give up the profession and in 1911 he published his first novel, *The White Peacock*. The following year he eloped to

Germany with his former tutor's wife, Frieda Weekley, and the couple married in 1914 after her divorce. The same year, Lawrence's collection of short stories, *The Prussian Officer*, was published.

Lawrence's poor health meant that he was declared unfit for military service and he spent the duration of the First World War in England, completing two of his most famous novels, *The Rainbow* (1915) and *Women in Love* (1916, published 1921).

After the war, Lawrence and his wife began to travel the world, searching for a more natural alternative to the industrialised lifestyle of the West. Until his early death from tuberculosis in Venice in 1930, Lawrence produced a vast quantity of work, including poetry, fiction, essays and travel writing; however, its worth was not fully appreciated until years after his death.

Lawrence wrote a small number of supernatural short stories, several of which first appeared in Lady Cynthia Asquith's popular series of ghost anthologies.

The most famous of these, *The Rocking Horse Winner* (1926), was a last minute contribution to replace the tale, *Glad Ghosts* (1926), which Lawrence withdrew due to the close resemblance of one of the main characters to Asquith herself. Lawrence's ghost stories are all very different, and it is difficult to identify common themes.

It is interesting that such an avant-garde author found the somewhat conservative supernatural genre a useful vehicle for his ideas; perhaps the irrational nature of the subject matter appealed to Lawrence as a further reaction against increasingly scientific Western civilisation.

Selected bibliography

The New Decameron: the Fourth Volume Edited by Wilfred Blair and containing stories by J. D. Beresford, Blair, Horace Horsnell, Storm Jameson, Robert Kenble, D.H. Lawrence, Edgill Rickword, Michael Sadleir, L.A.G. Strong. Oxford: Basil Blackwell, 1925.
This includes the first appearance of Lawrence's supernatural tale, The Last Laugh, *here printed with the title,* The Tale of the lady of Fashion: The Last Laugh.

The Ghost Book: Sixteen New Stories of the Uncanny Compiled by Lady Cynthia Asquith. London: Hutchinson and Co. (Publishers) Ltd., 1926.
This volume includes Lawrence's most frequently anthologised ghost story, The Rocking Horse Winner.

Glad Ghosts by D.H. Lawrence. London: Ernest Benn Limited, 1926.
Lawrence's ghost story was published in a limited edition of 500 copies as well as a popular paperback edition. The story was originally intended for Cynthia Asquith's classic collection, The Ghost Book *(1926) but withdrawn due to a character's resemblance to the anthologist.*

The Woman Who Rode Away and Other Stories by D.H. Lawrence. London: Martin Secker, 1928.
A general collection that includes two reprinted ghost stories, Glad Ghosts *and* The Last Laugh *together with a new supernatural story,* The Border Line.

W. Somerset Maugham (1874-1965)

William Somerset Maugham was born in Paris but moved to England to live with an uncle and aunt in Kent after losing his parents at the age of ten. Although he trained as a doctor at London's St Thomas' Hospital, Maugham soon gave up medicine to concentrate on his first love, writing.

Following some experimentation with mainstream fiction, his first real literary success came as a dramatist, with the humorous stage play, *Lady Frederick* (1907). It was not until 1915 that Maugham's talents as a fiction writer were recognized by a wide audience when his semi-autobiographical novel, *Of Human Bondage*, was published.

Maugham continued to work as a playwright and novelist, consolidating a reputation as one of the foremost British writers of his generation, and accomplishing the rare feat of achieving commercial success with works of high literary merit.

Maugham's most significant supernatural work is his novel, *The Magician* (1908), based on his encounters with the infamous occultist and author, Aleister Crowley, with whom he boarded briefly in Paris. The story's central character, a thinly disguised portrait of Crowley, attempts to achieve divine status through the use of black magic and human sacrifice.

The events portrayed in the story undoubtedly added to the body of myth and half-truth so carefully fostered by Crowley himself, and which led the British press to brand him the 'wickedest man in the world'. The novel is an interesting and imaginative foray into the supernatural, although it does not match the high standard of Maugham's more mature mainstream work.

In addition to *The Magician*, Maugham sometimes used supernatural subjects in his numerous short stories, most notably the regularly anthologised oriental tale of terror, *The Taipan*.

Selected bibliography

On a Chinese Screen by W. Somerset Maugham. London: William Heinemann, 1922.
This work comprises short sketches of life in China and includes Maugham's most famous supernatural short story, The Taipan.

Shudders: A Collection of New Nightmare Tales Compiled by Cynthia Asquith. London: Hutchinson & Co. (Publishers) Ltd., 1929.
This includes Maugham's supernatural tale, The End of the Flight.

Creatures of Circumstance by W. Somerset Maugham. London: William Heinemann, 1947.
A mainstream short story collection, including a single ghost story, A Man from Glasgow.

The Magician by William Somerset Maugham. London: William Heinemann, 1908.
A semi-autobiographical occult novel based on Maugham's early life in Paris and featuring a character modelled on Aleister Crowley. The novel, although interesting from a supernatural genre viewpoint, is not one of the author's best works.

Hector Hugh Munro (1870-1916

(Pseudonym: Saki)

Hector Hugh Munro was born in Burma, but sent to England following his mother's death to receive a strict Victorian upbringing under the care of two aunts. As a young man, Munro returned to Burma and joined the military police but was forced to return to England a year later after contracting malaria.

Following his recovery, Munro decided to pursue a career as a journalist and joined *The Westminster Gazette* in 1896 as a political satirist. He rapidly gained a reputation for his piercing wit and in 1902 moved to the *Morning Post* as a foreign correspondent. During this period, Munro also perfected his skills as a short story writer and published his first successful collection, *Reginald*, in 1904.

Adopting the pen name 'Saki', Munro went on to become one of the most admired short story writers of his generation, producing a series of highly successful collections memorable for their malevolent wit and extraordinary plot twists. Munro served in World War One, refusing a commission, and was killed in action in 1916.

Munro's treatment of the supernatural is highly distinctive, elegantly combining elements of humour and horror with an often sadistic glee. His targets are frequently members of the English upper class who encounter an uncontrollable natural or supernatural force and suffer disastrous but cruelly appropriate consequences.

Munro frequently drew on his travel experiences as a foreign correspondent to incorporate folk legends and motifs from around the world into his work. Often fatalistic, his fiction is particularly notable for its lack of sentiment at a time when over-sentimentality was an all too common trademark of popular fiction.

On occasion, the author seems to relish the suffering he inflicts on unfortunate characters, guilty and innocent alike, an unpleasant trait which sometimes compromises the overall success of his fiction.

Selected bibliography

Reginald in Russia and Other Sketches by Saki (H. H. Munro). London: Methuen & Co., 1910.
A classic mainstream short story collection which contains one of Saki's best known supernatural tales, Gabriel-Ernest, *plus a further ghostly piece,* The Soul of Laploshka.

The Chronicles of Clovis by H.H. Munro ('Saki'). London: John Lane, The Bodley Head; New York: John Lane Company, 1912.
This is Saki's best short story collection and includes two supernatural tales, the popular The Music on the Hill *and a lesser known tale,* The Peace of Mowsle Barton.

Beasts and Super-Beasts by H.H. Munro ('Saki'). London: John Lane The Bodley Head; New York: John Lane Company; Toronto: Bell & Cockburn, 1914.
A high quality mainstream collection of short stories which contains one of the few highly successful humorous tales of the supernatural, the much anthologised story, The Open Window.

The Toys of Peace and Other Papers by H.H. Munro ('Saki') with a portrait and a memoir. London: John Lane, The Bodley Head; New York: John Lane Company, 1919.
A posthumous collection of short stories, including two supernatural tales, The Hedgehog, *and* The Wolves of Cernogratz.

The Square Egg and Other Sketches, with Three Plays and Illustrations by H.H. Munro ('Saki') with a Biography by his Sister. London: John Lane The Bodley Head Limited, 1924.
This final posthumous collection of Saki's miscellaneous fiction includes one supernatural tale, The Infernal Parliament.

J.B. Priestley (1894-1984)

John Boynton Priestley was born in Bradford, and graduated from Cambridge University to become a prolific essayist and writer of literary reviews. His talent for writing fiction was first recognised by the public on the publication of his third novel, *The Good Companions* (1929).

A highly versatile writer, Priestley achieved success in several literary forms. As a dramatist, he was noted for his series of plays about the nature of time as well as his popular comedies. He also wrote non-fiction works on history, travel and philosophy.

During the Second World War, Priestley developed a new career as a broadcaster, creating a series of popular radio essays, many of which were eventually published in book form. In later years, when his output of fiction dwindled, Priestley produced several highly regarded volumes of autobiography.

Priestley's supernatural works are, like much of his fiction, heavily influenced by the 'Serial Time' theories of the philosopher J. W. Dunne. This is why Priestley's ghosts are equally likely to originate in a potential future or a dead past. His characters may even find themselves transported into the past to be perceived as ghosts themselves.

Fortunately, Priestley's sophisticated narrative skills and deft use of dark humour allow him to incorporate the essence of Dunne's complex theories without significantly disrupting the flow of his plots.

Due to their often unconventional subject matter, Priestley's tales have regularly appeared in genre fiction anthologies as well as more mainstream collections. While not a writer of traditional ghost stories, Priestley's work is of considerable interest to readers of supernatural fiction and repays careful attention.

Selected bibliography

The Other Place and Other Stories of the Same Sort by J.B. Priestley. Melbourne, London: William Heinemann Ltd., 1953.
A collection of assorted fantasy short stories about the nature of time and reality. Uncle Phil on TV *contains possibly the first haunted television to feature in supernatural literature. An original and interesting collection.*

The Carfitt Crisis, and Two Other Stories by J.B. Priestley. London: Heinemann, 1975.

A mainstream short story collection, including one supernatural fantasy, Underground.

The Magicians by J.B. Priestley. Melbourne, London: William Heinemann Ltd., 1954.
An unusual occult adventure novel about the nature of time.

Sir Arthur Thomas Quiller-Couch (1863-1944)
(Pseudonym: Q)

Born in Bodmin, Cornwall, Arthur Quiller-Couch was educated at Oxford University where he laid the foundations for a long and successful academic career, eventually becoming Professor of English Literature at Cambridge University.

During his time at Cambridge, Quiller-Couch comprehensively revised the English curriculum to give it a more contemporary emphasis. He was knighted in 1910 in recognition of his academic work and two of his lecture series of the period, *The Art of Writing* (1916) and *The Art of Reading* (1920), were published to considerable critical acclaim.

Quiller-Couch edited several important works, most notably *The Oxford Book of English Verse* (1902), which remained the definitive anthology of English poetry for much of the twentieth century.

The bulk of Quiller-Couch's prodigious output of fiction was produced early in his career and published under his 'Q' pseudonym. Much of this work has a historical theme and frequently draws on the legends and folklore of his native Cornwall. Quiller-Couch's first significant success came with *Dead Man's Rock* (1887), an adventure novel notable for its effective macabre episodes.

His ghost stories are scattered throughout his numerous short story collections, but *Q's Mystery Stories* (1937), provides a useful sampler of his best genre work.

Quiller-Couch is a master stylist, and his ghost stories are memorable for their subtlety, skilful handling of atmosphere and careful plot development. Several of the stories, including *The Roll-Call of the Reef* (1895) and *A Pair of Hands* (1900), have become classics and are regularly included in supernatural fiction anthologies.

Selected bibliography

I Saw Three Ships, and Other Winter's Tales by Q. London: Cassell & Company Limited, 1892.
A mainstream collection that contains Quiller-Couch's successful ghost story, The Haunted Dragoon, *together with a lesser tale,* A Blue Pantomime. *The author also wrote the words of the famous Christmas carol which shares the name of this collection.*

Wandering Heath: Stories, Studies, and Sketches by Q. London: Cassell and Company Limited, 1895.
A collection of Cornish tales, including Quiller-Couch's most anthologised supernatural tale, The Roll-Call of the Reef. *Ghosts are depicted in* My Grandfather, Hendry Watty, *but the situation turns out to be a dream.*

Old Fires and Profitable Ghosts: A Book of Stories by A. T. Quiller-Couch. London: Cassell and Company

Limited, 1900.

A mainstream collection that includes some excellent supernatural tales, most notably, The Seventh Man *and the justly famous,* A Pair of Hands.

Merry-Garden and Other Stories by 'Q' (A.T. Quiller-Couch). London: Methuen & Co., 1907.

A mainstream short story collection containing one effective ghostly tale, The Bend of the Road.

Sir Walter Scott (1771-1832)

Born in Edinburgh, Walter Scott trained as a lawyer before gaining a literary reputation for his translations of German Romantic poetry. The success inspired Scott to publish his own work and he gradually became a considerable influence on the European Romantic movement, a position which allowed him to assist several young writers, including James Hogg, at the start of their careers.

Although it was his skills as a translator and poet that first brought Scott to public attention, his lasting legacy was the popularisation of historical fiction through works such as *The Antiquary* (1816) and *The Heart of Midlothian* (1818).

The historical novel was highly esteemed throughout the nineteenth century by writers and the public alike and Scott's *Waverley* novels were seen as models of the genre. Royal recognition of Scott's literary achievement came when he was created a baronet in 1820. It is likely that overwork, brought on by attempts to clear his debts following a series of financial disasters, hastened his death in 1832.

Much of Scott's work is concerned with the supernatural and even his historical novels, such as *Redgauntlet* (1824), include ghostly incidents. An early poem, *Glenfinlas*, was included in *Tales of Wonder* (1801), a collection of supernatural literature assembled by Matthew 'Monk' Lewis, one of the founders of English Gothic fiction.

Scott also studied Scottish witchcraft and recorded his findings in one of his final works, *Letters on Demonology and Witchcraft* (1830). Scott's ghost stories are of an extremely high standard and like those of his protégé, James Hogg, were largely inspired by Scottish folklore. In particular, *The Two Drovers* from *Chronicles of the Canongate* (1827), has long been regarded as one of the finest examples of the short story form published in the nineteenth century.

Scott's stories were an important influence on writers of the Victorian ghost story and mark the beginning of the transition from the Gothic tradition to the more naturalistic style of later writers such as Charles Dickens. Scott outlined his views on the creation of ghostly works in an essay, *On the Supernatural in Fictitious Composition, and Particularly on the Works of E.T.A. Hoffman*, published in *The Foreign Quarterly Review* in 1827.

Selected bibliography

Redgauntlet: A Tale of the Eighteenth Century by the Author of 'Waverley' in Three Volumes. Edinburgh: Archibald Constable and Co., 1824.

This includes a self-contained ghost story, Wandering Willies Tale, *one of the high points of early nineteenth century supernatural fiction. The story has also appeared in anthologies as* The Feast of Redgauntlet, The Devil's Receipt, and, A Night in the Grave, *the latter being a slightly revised version of the work.*

Chronicles of the Canongate by the Author of 'Waverley' etc. in Two Volumes. Edinburgh: Cadell and Co.; London: Simpkin and Marshall, 1827.
A general collection containing one of Scott's most popular supernatural tales, The Two Drovers, *as part of chapter 13. Chapter 8 consists of a long borderline piece,* The Highland Widow. *The introduction is signed Walter Scott.*

The Keepsake for MDCCCXXIX edited by Frederic Mansel Reynolds. London: Published for the Proprietor, by Hurst, Chance and Co., 1828.
This includes two excellent ghost stories by Scott, My Aunt Margaret's Mirror *and* The Tapestried Chamber, *or* The Lady in the Sacque. *The former tale has also been anthologised as* The Tale of the Mysterious Mirror *and* The Mirror, *both attributed to the 'author of Waverly'.*

Letters on Demonology and Witchcraft, Addressed to J. G. Lockhart, Esq. by Sir Walter Scott. London: John Murray, 1830.
This comprises Scott's thoughts on these subjects gleaned from his research into Scottish folklore. Since its publication, several sections of the work have appeared as self-contained stories in supernatural fiction anthologies under a variety of titles, including The Ghost of Sergeant Davies, The Letters on Demonology and Witchcraft, The Mystery of Glamis, The Phantom Chief *and* The Witches of Auldearne. *The*

work is illustrated with plates designed by George Cruikshank.

The Supernatural Short Stories of Sir Walter Scott Edited by Michael Hayes. London: John Calder, 1977. *This is a useful reprint collection of Scott's ghost stories.*

Robert Louis Stevenson (1850-1894)

Robert Louis Stevenson was born in Edinburgh and educated at the city's university. When ill health prevented a plan to follow his father into engineering, he chose to study law and was called to the bar in 1875. However, he never practised and instead journeyed widely through Europe and America, using his experiences as material for the travel books that were his first published work.

Stevenson's early writing, including children's essays and plays, earned him little attention, but fame eventually came with the publication of two now classic works, *Treasure Island* (1883) and *The Strange Case of Dr Jekyll and Mr Hyde* (1886). Although the self-deprecating Stevenson once dismissed the latter work as his 'shilling shocker', he is now recognised as having significantly raised the literary standard of popular macabre and adventure fiction of the period.

Continuing ill health dogged Stevenson throughout his short life, but did not prevent him travelling extensively in a quest to gain new experiences and further material for his work. He eventually chose to make his home at Molokai, in Samoa, where his health briefly improved before his death from tuberculosis at the age of 44. His final work *Island Nights* (1893), written in Samoa, drew heavily on local legends to produce some highly original fantasy tales.

A master story teller, Stevenson was fascinated by the supernatural and human reactions to it, sometimes referring to his more horrific tales as 'crawlers'. He applied the same high standards to his supernatural and horror works as he brought to his adventure fiction and wrote a series of original genre stories with widely varying subject matter.

Several tales explore the author's life-long fascination with the duality of human nature, most famously *The Strange Case of Dr Jekyll and Mr Hyde*. This theme also appears to a lesser degree in some of Stevenson's other novels such as *Deacon Brodie* (1879) and *The Master of Ballantrae* (1889). The latter work was the result of a collaboration between Stevenson and his step-son, Lloyd Osborne. The pair also worked together on *The Wrong Box* (1889), a humorous novel with some supernatural features.

Selected bibliography

The Merry Men and Other Tales and Fables by Robert Louis Stevenson. London: Chatto & Windus, 1887. *A collection of original tales, including some of Stevenson's most effective supernatural work.*

Island Nights' Entertainments: consisting of The Beach of Falesá, The Bottle Imp, The Isle of Voices by Robert Louis Stevenson with Illustrations by Gordon Browne and W. Hatherell. London: Cassell & Company Limited, 1893.

An excellent collection of supernatural fantasies, including The Bottle Imp *based on Samoan legends. The work is illustrated by Gordon Browne.*

The Strange Case of Dr. Jekyll and Mr. Hyde, with Other Fables by Robert Louis Stevenson. London: Longmans, Green & Co. 1896.
In addition to Jekyll, *this volume includes a series of very short fantasy and supernatural sketches.* The Strange Case of Dr. Jekyll and Mr. Hyde *was first published in 1886 and referred to by Stevenson as his 'shilling shocker'. It has some supernatural touches, but is closer to science fiction than the ghost genre.*

Tales and Fantasies by Robert Louis Stevenson. London: Chatto & Windus, 1905.
This includes Stevenson's famous tale, The Body-Snatcher, *which had originally appeared in* The Pall Mall Christmas Extra *in 1884.*

The Supernatural Short Stories of Robert Louis Stevenson edited by Michael Hayes. London: John Calder, 1976.
A useful single volume collection of Stevenson's ghostly work.

H.G. Wells (1866-1946)

Herbert George Wells was born in Bromley, Kent, the son of a shopkeeper. Wells was apprenticed to a draper in his early teens, but later continued his education and studied under the prominent Darwinist, Thomas Henry Huxley, at London University. Wells was greatly influenced by Huxley and much of his early fiction explores the implications of Darwinian theory for the future evolution of the human race.

Wells' scientific essays and short stories began to appear in periodicals from 1893, but it was his first novel, *The Time Machine* (1895), that established him as a founding father of science fiction. This seminal work was followed in 1898 by *The War of the Worlds*, the first significant novel to depict an alien invasion of Earth.

Before the First World War, much of Wells' writing is optimistic in tone, promoting the Victorian ideal of progress via technology. From 1903, following his conversion to socialism, Wells' novels begin to contain more overtly social or political themes exploring possible utopias and the nature of the English class system.

However, after the First World War, aspects of which he accurately predicted in several of his works, Wells became increasingly disillusioned and pessimistic about human society. Nevertheless, he continued to be a prolific writer, producing non-fiction, including the highly successful *The Outline of History* (1920), together with influential science fiction, such as *The Shape of Things to Come* (1933), but he never again recaptured the vitality of his earlier work.

At first glance, it may seem strange for such a formidable champion of scientific rationalism to write in the supernatural and fantasy genres. However, Wells saw the potential in both to further explore one of his favourite themes, that of making the seemingly impossible possible.

While his science fiction work frequently includes the

invention of some revolutionary technology, his fantasies often call on some form of supernatural or religious intervention, for example, the concept of reincarnation in *The Dream* (1924). Although Wells produced very few traditional ghost stories, *The Red Room* (1896) is widely acknowledged as a classic of the genre and regularly appears in supernatural fiction anthologies.

Selected bibliography

The Stolen Bacillus and Other Incidents by H.G. Wells. London: Methuen & Co., 1895.
An excellent science fiction and fantasy collection, including several supernatural and borderline supernatural items, most notably The Temptation of Harringay *and* A Moth – Genus Novo.

The Plattner Story and Others by H.G. Wells. London: Methuen & Co., 1897.
A miscellaneous collection of fantasy, science fiction and supernatural tales, including Wells' most anthologised and most traditional ghost story, The Red Room, *which has also been reprinted as* The Ghost of Fear.

The Country of the Blind and Other Stories by H.G. Wells. London: Thomas Nelson and Sons, 1911.
This is Wells' own selection of his best short stories and includes his popular supernatural fantasy, The Door in the Wall.

The Croquet Player: A Story by H.G. Wells. London: Chatto & Windus, 1936.
This long, allegorical ghost story, set in the East Anglian Fens, is one of Wells' most effective final works.

Oscar Wilde (1854-1900)

Oscar Fingal O'Flahertie Wills Wilde was born in Dublin and educated at the city's Trinity College, and then Magdalen College, Oxford. It was at Oxford that Wilde gained attention as a leader of the 'aesthetic' movement and began to develop a reputation for his intellect and wit.

Although Wilde published a volume of poems in 1882, his literary career did not really take off until after his marriage to Constance Lloyd in 1884. A book of fairy tales, *The Happy Prince* (1888), was well received, but it was Wilde's novel, *The Picture of Dorian Gray* (1890), that brought him both acclaim and considerable disapproval for its ambiguous moral stance.

Wilde followed this success with a popular series of sophisticated plays, including *Lady Windermere's Fan* (1892), *A Woman of No Importance* (1893) and *The Importance of Being Earnest* (1895). However, Wilde's drama, *Salome* (1894), was banned by the Lord Chamberlain and received its first performance in Paris. Wilde's relationship with the play's translator, Lord Alfred Douglas, led to his conviction and imprisonment for homosexuality followed by public disgrace. After completing his prison sentence, he moved to France where he lived until his early death in 1900.

Wilde produced two classic tales of the supernatural, *The Picture of Dorian Gray* (1890) and *The Canterville Ghost* (1891) both of which remain popular today and have been regularly adapted for film and television. The works share little in common apart from Wilde's sparkling prose style: *The Picture of Dorian Gray* is the darker and more serious piece, exploring the role of morality in the life of the artist, while *The Canterville Ghost* skilfully lampoons the haunted house tales of previous generations.

The Picture of Dorian Gray excited considerable contemporary controversy, being considered inspirational by the Decadent movement, but highly immoral by more traditional members of Victorian society. Over a century later, it still ranks as one of the most original British supernatural novels ever written.

Selected bibliography

Lord Arthur Savile's Crime & Other Stories by Oscar Wilde. London: James R. Osgood, McIlvaine and Co., 1891.
This includes two supernatural items, Lord Arthur Savile's Crime, *which deals with fortune telling, and* The Canterville Ghost, *one of the rare examples of a successful humorous ghost story. The latter has been adapted many times for film, television and radio.*

The Picture of Dorian Gray and Other Writings by Oscar Wilde; Edited with an Introduction by Richard Ellmann. Toronto, New York, London: Bantam Books, 1982.
This is a modern corrected edition of this fascinating novel which seasons passages of subtle horror with sparkling aphorisms; one of the few examples of supernatural fiction to have passed into popular culture. This edition includes a useful introduction by Wilde's biographer, Richard Ellmann.

The Mystery of 'B'

Between 1911 and 1914, a number of fine antiquarian ghost stories were published in the pages of the *Magdalene College Magazine*, appearing under the pseudonym 'B'. The identity of the author remains a mystery to this day. Various names have been put forward over the years, including E.G. Swain, Arthur Gray and A.C. Benson.

Leaving the question of authorship to one side, it is generally agreed that the stories may have been created in response to Gray's 'Ingulphus' ghost series about the history of Jesus College, Cambridge.

Heavily influenced by the ghost story master, M.R. James, the tales combine scholarship with a careful use of atmosphere and a fine sense of humour. A rapid evolution in the sophistication of the writer's technique is evident when the dates of the individual tales are compared.

Five of the stories were collected by the anthologist Rosemary Pardoe and published in 1986 under her Haunted Library imprint.

A further tale by 'B', *The Hare*, was included in the Haunted Library magazine, *Ghosts and Scholars* (no. 8), in 1986. The remaining story in the series, *The Stone Coffin*, featured in Richard Dalby and Rosemary Pardoe's anthology, *Ghosts and Scholars*, published in 1987.

Short stories by 'B'

The Hole in the Wall
Quia Nominor
The Stone Coffin
The Strange Case of Mr Naylor
The Strange Fate of Mr Peach
When the Door is Shut

Unsettling Tales: A Suggested Reading List

Are your doors locked? Have you pulled the curtains across the darkened window? Do you have a comfy chair, cosy fire and glass of something to hand? Excellent. Now prepare to be unsettled and disturbed by these outstanding examples of supernatural fiction.

But wait... listen... was that a footstep on the stair? Did the lights just flicker? Or was it just your imagination... ?

E.F. Benson

Caterpillars
Mrs Amworth

Algernon Blackwood

The Empty House
The Willows

Elizabeth Bowen

The Demon Lover

Walter de la Mare

All Hallows

Robert Hichens

How Love Came to Professor Guildea

M.R. James

A Neighbour's Landmark
The Ash Tree

Sheridan Le Fanu

Green Tea

Arthur Machen

The Red Hand
The Novel of the Black Seal

Oliver Onions

The Rope in the Rafters
The Beckoning Fair One

L.T.C. Rolt

The Mine

May Sinclair

Where Their Fire Is Not Quenched

H.G. Wells

The Red Room

A Female Perspective

Introduction

During what came to be regarded as the golden age of the Victorian ghost story (1820-1950), bestselling authors such as Charlotte Riddell, Margaret Oliphant and Amelia Edwards created some of the most successful and satisfying ghost stories ever written, rich in nuanced ambiguity and psychological insight. They continued an important female contribution to the genre which began during the Gothic era with authors such as Ann Radcliffe and continued into the twentieth and twenty-first centuries with the works of Edith Nesbit and Susan Hill.

Many of the female authors included in this section led fascinating and occasionally very sad lives, and much of their work is now unjustly neglected or forgotten. This is our huge loss.

These brief biographies include many of the female writers who contributed to the British ghost story tradition, several of whom are now considered to be among the best authors in the genre. Here, for example, you will find E. Nesbit, famous today as the author of the perennially popular novel, *The Railway Children*. Nesbit claimed to have lived in at least two haunted houses as a child and along with her more famous works, wrote a number of excellent ghost stories.

Other entries include the mysterious Lettice Galbraith about whom little is known, but whose ghost story fiction is regarded by some as among the best ever written. Cynthia Asquith led a far less anonymous life, mixing with the leading literary figures of her day and cajoling or persuading authors such as D.H. Lawrence and L.P. Hartley to contribute ghost stories to her anthologies. She was also an accomplished writer in the genre herself.

You can also discover Dorothy Macardle, a prominent figure in Irish literary society, who wrote her first ghost stories while in prison in 1922 for nationalist activities, as well as the wonderfully named Wilhelmina Fitzclarence, Countess of Munster who published her first book when she was nearly sixty.

Other fascinating characters include Lady Eleanor Furneaux Smith, the daughter of the Earl of Birkenhead, who joined a circus in an attempt to experience a wandering gypsy lifestyle, and Mary Mackay, who adopted the stage name Marie Corelli early in life while working as a musician. Mackay became Britain's most commercially successful novelist of the period, counting Queen Victoria among her admirers. However, as her popularity diminished she went into a sad decline, ultimately losing touch with reality.

Here too are Emily and Charlotte Brontë, included for Emily's creation of one of the most famous ghosts in all of literature, and Charlotte for a very early ghostly tale as well as the supernatural elements that permeate much of her mature writing. Also listed is another leading literary figure, Elizabeth Bowen, who despite having produced a relatively small number of ghostly tales is widely regarded as one of the genre's most sophisticated writers.

These are just a few examples of the female authors included here, many of whom still await rediscovery and the recognition they so richly deserve.

DB

Lady Cynthia Mary Evelyn Asquith (1887-1960)

Cynthia Asquith was one of the supernatural genre's most important anthologists. As wife of the poet Herbert Asquith and secretary to the playwright J.M. Barrie, Asquith mixed with many of the established and rising literary figures of her time.

She commissioned eminent writers such as D.H. Lawrence, Hugh Walpole and L.P. Hartley to contribute new stories to her series of ghost story anthologies. Many tales now acknowledged as classics of the genre first appeared in her highly popular collections.

A lifelong ghost story enthusiast, Asquith was also an accomplished author in her own right, writing mostly biographies and children's fiction.

However, Asquith also wrote some fine supernatural short stories, several of which first appeared in her own anthologies. Asquith's ghost stories might more accurately be described as macabre tragedies in which the living and the dead relive past horrors together.

In contrast to the prevailing style of the time, Asquith's ghosts are less ambiguous and often have carefully drawn personalities to allow a more complex and satisfying interaction with her living protagonists.

Selected bibliography

The Ghost Book: Sixteen New Stories of the Uncanny Compiled by Lady Cynthia Asquith. London: Hutchinson and Co. (Publishers) Ltd., 1926.
One of the supernatural genre's best collections, reprinted numerous times. In addition to editing this work, Asquith contributed one tale, The Corner Shop, *under the pseudonym C.L. Ray.*

Shudders: A Collection of New Nightmare Tales Compiled by Cynthia Asquith. London: Hutchinson & Co. (Publishers) Ltd., 1929.
A collection of high quality supernatural and horror tales assembled by Asquith and including her own story, The Playfellow.

What Dreams May Come by Cynthia Asquith. London: James Barrie, 1951.
Asquith's collection of her own short stories is dedicated to L.P. Hartley and includes several tales previously published in her own anthologies. The collection first appeared in America as This Mortal Coil *(Sauk City: Arkham House, 1947).*

Diaries 1915-1918 by Lady Cynthia Asquith; with a Foreword by L.P. Hartley. London: Hutchinson of London, 1968.
Asquith's diaries offer an intimate and fascinating insight into her leisured lifestyle as well as that of her many friends in literature and politics.

Louisa Baldwin (1845-1925)

(Mrs Alfred Baldwin)

Louisa Baldwin (née MacDonald) was at the heart of late Victorian and Edwardian political and artistic society; her celebrated relations included her brother-in-law the artist Edward Byrne-Jones and her nephew Rudyard Kipling. Her marriage to Alfred Baldwin, the politician and industrialist, produced a son, Stanley, who later became Prime Minister.

Baldwin was a prolific writer of fiction and poetry and frequent contributor to numerous Victorian short story magazines. Although much of her work was later published in book form, it is likely that further pieces await rediscovery.

Following the tradition developed by Charles Dickens and others, many of Baldwin's ghost stories were contributed to Christmas numbers. While some of her tales are over-sentimental in a manner typical of the Victorian era, most have aged well and several are included in more recent anthologies.

Selected bibliography

The Shadow on the Blind and Other Ghost Stories by Mrs Alfred Baldwin. London: J. M. Dent & Co., 1895. *A fine collection of mid-Victorian ghost stories which is dedicated to Baldwin's nephew, Rudyard Kipling.*

Elizabeth Bowen (1899-1973)

Elizabeth Dorothea Cole Bowen was born in Dublin, but her father's ill health meant she spent much of her childhood with various relatives in England. The recurrent themes of loneliness and the disintegration of family bonds found in much of her work doubtless had their roots in this unhappy period.

Bowen achieved her first literary success as a writer of short stories, publishing the collection, *Encounters*, in 1923. A novel, *The Hotel*, followed in 1927, and she also worked as an essayist and biographer. However, it was Bowen's fiction that contributed most to her growing reputation, its fine craftsmanship being coupled with a rare emotional depth and sensitivity, as in the successful novels, *The Death of the Heart* (1938) and *The Heat of the Day* (1949).

While Bowen did not believe the novel an appropriate literary form for the exploration of supernatural themes, her writing often implies the unreality of ordinary experience. However, she did successfully tackle the subject in several short stories which are widely considered important contributions to the genre. An interesting feature of some of Bowen's tales is the combination of folk motifs and elements of traditional ghost fiction within a contemporary urban setting. The author's subtle treatment of the nature of time and human fear probably reflects her experiences during the London Blitz as much as her disrupted childhood.

Bowen's interest in the ghost story form is reflected both in the preface to her own short story collections and in her introduction to Cynthia Asquith's anthology, *The Second Ghost Book* (1952). Bowen wrote a relatively small number of ghost stories, but they were of such a high standard that she is widely regarded as one of the genre's most sophisticated and mature writers.

Selected bibliography

The Demon Lover and Other Stories by Elizabeth Bowen. London: Jonathan Cape, 1945.
A general collection containing much supernatural material heavily influenced by Bowen's wartime experiences. Published in America under the title Ivy Gripped the Steps.

A Day in the Dark and Other Stories by Elizabeth Bowen. London: Jonathan Cape, c1965.
A collection of Bowen's best short stories containing an interesting preface by the author commenting on the use of supernatural themes in her work.

M.E. Braddon (1835-1915)

Mary Elizabeth Braddon was one of the most popular novelists of her day. She first achieved bestseller status with *Lady Audley's Secret* (1862), a controversial novel of modern' morality that scandalised polite society, bringing the author a notoriety that helped boost her sales.

Best known for her sensational and romantic fiction, Braddon also included mystery, comedy and the supernatural among her output of more than eighty books. Although she counted Thackeray among her many admirers and was considered an important literary figure, Braddon's work was uneven in quality. This was doubtless due to the demands of maintaining her prodigious output while also working as an editor for popular magazines. Two of these periodicals, *Temple Bar* and *Belgravia*, saw the first, often anonymous, publication of much of her work.

Braddon's supernatural fiction is considered to be among her strongest, but modern readers may find many of her stories excessively melodramatic and riddled with the tired motifs of the Gothic genre, albeit in updated settings.

However, her best tales demonstrate a deeper psychological insight and are skilfully constructed. Several of Braddon's most successful tales, such as *The Cold Embrace*, have been regularly anthologised.

Selected bibliography

Ralph the Bailiff and Other Tales by M.E. Braddon. London: Ward and Lock, 1862. (The Shilling Volume Library)
A collection of solid mid-Victorian commercial fiction, including some supernatural material. The work includes one of Braddon's most regularly anthologised stories, The Cold Embrace. *An expanded edition of this collection was published in 1869 and included two further stories:* Eveline's Visitant *and* How I Heard My Own Will Read, *the latter being a 'hideous dream' rather than supernatural.*

Dracula's Brood: Rare Vampire Stories by Friends and Contemporaries of Bram Stoker Selected and Introduced by Richard Dalby. Wellingborough: Crucible, 1987.
Braddon's tale, The good Lady Ducayne, *is about a young girl who takes a job with a female vampire. The story first*

appeared in Strand Magazine *in 1895 and therefore pre-dated the publication of Bram Stoker's* Dracula.

Charlotte Brontë (1816-1855)

As a child, Charlotte Brontë, together with her brother and sisters, read numerous Gothic and supernatural tales in the pages of the famous *Blackwood's Edinburgh Magazine*. These stories, coupled with the winter gloom of her family home at Haworth, may have helped inspire the young Brontë to write her early ghost tale, *Napoleon and the Spectre* in 1833. The work remained unpublished until 1919.

A more significant treatment of the supernatural can be found in two of the author's most famous novels. *Jane Eyre* (1847) is permeated with uncanny events which are later rationalised, while *Villette* (1853) includes the appearances of a female ghost.

Predominantly, however, Brontë treats her macabre subjects with a touch of scepticism and a character in her novel *Shirley* (1849) actually mocks the excesses of the traditional Gothic novel, voicing opinions which may well reflect the author's own.

Selected bibliography

Napoleon and the Spectre: A Ghost Story by Charlotte Brontë. London: Privately printed by Clement Shorter, February 1919.
A short piece of supernatural juvenilia written when Brontë was 17 years old. The volume is part of a limited edition of twenty-five copies privately printed for distribution among the publisher's

friends. The story was later included in a more accessible collection, The Twelve Adventurers *(Hodder & Stoughton, 1925).*

Villette by Currer Bell in Three Volumes. London: Smith, Elder & Co, 1853.
A classic mainstream novel featuring ghostly manifestations written under Brontë's 'Currer Bell' pseudonym.

Emily Brontë (1818-1848)

Emily Jane Brontë began writing as a child, working with her sisters and brother to create a complex web of stories and poems based on mythical worlds peopled by real and imaginary characters. Emily continued to add to this 'Gondal' cycle throughout her life, underlining the importance to her of the fictional world she and her siblings had created.

Emily died just a year after the publication of her only novel, *Wuthering Heights* (1847). *Wuthering Heights* provides a link between the Gothic tradition of the late eighteenth and early nineteenth centuries and the new, more naturalistic style of authors such as Mrs Gaskell.

The novel features stock Gothic motifs, including a crumbling ancestral home, dark family secrets, and a ghost tapping at the window, but these are carefully blended with elements of romanticism. The Byronic hero, Heathcliff, and the equally strong-willed heroine, Cathy, enact a passionate story of love beyond death which has retained its power to the present day.

While the supernatural content of *Wuthering Heights* is

relatively slight, the novel is important to the genre as it legitimised the subject for serious contemporary fiction during an era characterised by rising scientific rationalism.

Brontë also wrote a number of poems on macabre topics, including *The Horrors of Sleep* (1846).

Selected bibliography

Wuthering Heights: A Novel by Ellis Bell, in Three Volumes. London: Thomas Cautley Newby Publisher, 1847.
Wuthering Heights *features perhaps the most famous ghost outside the plays of William Shakespeare. Although billed as appearing in three volumes, the novel is actually complete in two, with* Agnes Grey *by Acton Bell (Anne Brontë) being the third.*

Dorothy Kathleen Broster (1877-1950)

Dorothy Broster, an Oxford University history graduate, wrote a series of historical novels that gained a considerable reputation for their accurate evocation of past times. A series of tales set in Scotland at the time of the Jacobite Rebellion were particularly highly regarded. However, Broster's work is little known today.

Broster's supernatural tales are interesting and well-executed works of some originality. As might be expected, she created convincing historical settings for her ghostly fiction but also gave meticulous attention to the essential feature of all effective ghost stories: a skilful development of atmosphere.

Selected bibliography

Great Short Stories of Detection, Mystery and Horror. Third Series Edited by Dorothy L. Sayers. London: Victor Gollancz Ltd., 1934.
Contains the first appearance of Broster's story, Couching at the Door, *which became the title story of her later collection.*

Couching at the Door by D. K. Broster. London: William Heinemann Ltd., 1942.
A rare short story collection of Broster's best work in the supernatural genre.

Rhoda Broughton (1840-1920)

Rhoda Broughton was well-known during the Victorian era as an author of witty social novels often set in the countryside. Some contemporary readers were scandalised by her characters' 'modern' dialogues, but Broughton received much useful support from her uncle by marriage, the writer Joseph Sheridan Le Fanu.

It was thanks to Le Fanu that Broughton's novel, *Not Wisely But Too Well* (1867) came to the attention of the publisher Bentley and Son. However, it was initially refused as too coarse for publication and it was not until her second novel, *Cometh Up as a Flower* (1867), proved such a commercial success that Bentley finally agreed to publish *Not Wisely But Too Well*. Bentley remained Broughton's publisher for the rest of her long writing career.

It was possibly Le Fanu who inspired his niece to try her hand at the ghost story genre that he had already so successfully mastered, and several of Broughton's stories first appeared in the pages of the popular *Temple Bar* magazine.

Although Broughton never matched her uncle's achievements, her stories are certainly above average, providing a skilful blend of traditional ghostly atmosphere with a level of psychological insight quite rare for the time.

Selected bibliography

Tales for Christmas Eve by Rhoda Broughton. London: Richard Bentley and Son, 1873.
A solid collection of traditional ghost stories for the festive season, later republished as Twilight Stories *(London: Richard Bentley and Son, 1879).*

Rhoda Broughton's Ghost Stories: and Other Tales of Mystery and Suspense with an Introduction by Marilyn Wood. Stamford: Paul Watkins, 1995.
A single volume collection of Broughton's supernatural work which includes three tales discovered in the Chester Record Office by Broughton's biographer Marilyn Wood.

Gabrielle Margaret Vere Campbell (1885-1952)
(Pseudonyms: Marjorie Bowen; Margaret Campbell; George R Preedy; Joseph Shearing; Robert Paye; John Winch)

Born on Hayling Island in Kent, Gabrielle Margaret Vere Campbell came from a family with a strong artistic tradition. Although Campbell briefly studied art in Paris, financial pressures led her to select the potentially more lucrative career of writing. Early success came in 1906 with the publication of her historical novel, *The Viper of Milan*.

A talented and imaginative author, Campbell wrote in many literary genres and styles, including crime fiction, children's stories and historical biographies, using a variety of pseudonyms. Although the author's most common pen name was Marjorie Bowen, she also published macabre material as George R. Preedy, Joseph Shearing, and Robert Paye.

A prolific writer and translator, Campbell produced over 170 novels, short story collections and non-fiction works in addition to editing several short story anthologies. Unfortunately, the pressure of meeting publishers' deadlines sometimes took its toll on the quality of Campbell's fiction, with many works well below the standard set by her best novels.

Uneven quality, coupled with the rarity of several of her best books, has often led to Campbell's supernatural work being undervalued. However, the author's better works exhibit skilful control of atmosphere, authentic historical background and highly original plots.

Campbell's often allegorical tales examine human fear from many viewpoints, blending horror and beauty or humour and tragedy in combinations that subtly evoke sympathy without sentimentality.

Selected bibliography

Orange Blossoms by Joseph Shearing. London:

William Heinemann Ltd., 1938.
A general collection which includes the excellent supernatural story, They Found My Grave.

Black Magic: A Tale of the Rise and Fall of Antichrist by Marjorie Bowen. London: Alston Rivers Ltd., 1909.
The author's most famous occult thriller. A historical work with considerable supernatural content set in the Middle Ages. Not, however, up to the standard of her later work.

Julia Roseingrave by Robert Paye. London: Ernest Benn Ltd, 1933.
An excellent witchcraft novel, arguably the author's best work in the genre.

The Fetch by Joseph Shearing. London: Hutchinson & Co. (Publishers) Ltd., 1942.
A well-written historical mystery about haunting and possession based on the original essay, The Ambiguities of Miss Smith, *by William Roughead. The work has also been issued under the title,* The Spectral Bride.

Great Tales of Horror: Being a Collection of Strange Stories of Amazement, Horror and Wonder, Selected, with an Introduction, by Marjorie Bowen. London: John Lane The Bodley Head Limited, 1933.
Includes the author's translations from the French (1812) of The Grey Chamber, The Dead Bride, *and* The Skull. *The preface discusses the merits of the modern ghost story.*

Agatha Christie (1890-1976)

Agatha Christie was born in Torquay, Devon, to an American father and English mother. She wrote her first novel, *The Mysterious Affair at Styles* (1930), while working in a Red Cross Hospital during the First World War: detective fiction would never be quite the same again.

Christie's interest in writing as a career was encouraged by a family friend and neighbour, the author Eden Phillpotts (1862-1960), and during her long career, Christie achieved a level of success in the crime fiction genre unknown since the days of the great Arthur Conan Doyle. A worldwide phenomenon, her works were translated into over one hundred languages. Even today it is rare for a month to pass without the broadcast of at least one of her plays, novels or short stories. Christie was awarded a CBE in 1951 for her contribution to English literature and was made a Dame Commander of the British Empire in 1971.

Before settling down to chronicle the exploits of characters such as Miss Marple and Hercule Poirot, Christie experimented with supernatural fiction in an early collection, *The Hound of Death and Other Stories* (1933).

The themes of justice and retribution found in her early writing were also explored in her later detective works. An attempt at fusing the ghost and crime genres through the character of a supernatural detective, Harley Quin, was not a great success, although Christie returned to the character several times during her writing career.

Her late novel, *By the Pricking of my Thumb* (1968), features some black magic as background material.

Selected bibliography

The Mysterious Mr Quin by Agatha Christie. London: W. Collins Sons & Co. Ltd., c1930.
A strange hybrid work in which crimes are solved via the intervention of Harley Quin, an ambiguous supernatural entity. Quin acts via a human intermediary and seems to be a personification of the spirit of justice.

The Hound of Death and Other Stories by Agatha Christie. London: Odhams Press Limited, c1933.
Often trawled by anthologists, this collection of well-written tales in both the detective and ghost genres is lacking in originality, although the supernatural tales are generally well handled. The main character in The Strange Case of Sir Andrew Carmichael *actually turns out to be called Arthur and in subsequent publications the story title is sometimes amended to correct this inconsistency. The collection is now chiefly remembered for the crime story,* A Witness for the Prosecution, *later successfully filmed.*

Miss Marple's Final Cases and Two Other Stories by Agatha Christie. London: Collins, 1979.
One of the two non-Marple stories, In a Glass Darkly, *is a supernatural tale.*

Bithia Mary Croker (1849-1920)

Born in County Roscommon, Ireland, as Bithia Mary Sheppard, Bithia Croker was a prolific writer of popular novels and short stories during the late nineteenth and early twentieth centuries. However, she is virtually unknown today.

Croker's supernatural stories are often hampered by an over-sentimental approach, characteristic of much popular literature of the time.

However, her use of unusual themes and exotic locations adds some interest and differentiates them from the clichéd haunted house stories so popular among pulp fiction writers of the period.

Selected bibliography

Number Ninety and Other Ghost Stories, by B.M. Croker. Welsh Sarob Press, 2000.
A limited edition collection of Croker's best supernatural work edited by Richard Dalby.

"To Let" etc. by B.M. Croker. London: Chatto & Windus, 1893.
A collection of rather dated and somewhat predictable stories of Anglo-Indian life. About half the collection has supernatural content.

Jason and Other Stories by B.M. Croker. London: Chatto & Windus, 1899.
A general collection, including the supernatural tales, Trooper Thompson's Information *and* Mrs Ponsonby's Dream.

Odds and Ends by B.M. Croker. London: Hutchinson & Co., 1919.
A very rare collection of stories varying greatly in subject and mood, set in Ireland and India. The work contains several supernatural stories, including The Creaking Board *which tells the story of a house that is haunted by the ghost of a ghost.*

Catherine Crowe (1790-1876)

Catherine Crowe was born in Borough Green, Kent, but moved to Edinburgh following her marriage in 1822. After a modest degree of success with potboiler fiction, Crowe achieved celebrity status with the publication of her collection of 'true' ghost tales *The Night Side of Nature* (1848). The author's transformation from writer of romantic fiction to ghost hunter can be traced to her translation of Justinus Kerner's bestselling factual work *The Seeress of Prevorst* in 1845.

Crowe was an early exponent of what would now be called faction, dramatising incidents of anecdote or folklore with a considerable degree of narrative skill. Her work was heavily influenced by her strong personal belief in the reality of spiritualism and it was this interest in the more morbid aspects of existence that friends blamed for her mental breakdown in the 1850s. Although Crowe recovered she wrote little more of significance before her death in 1876.

Over the years, Crowe's work has proved to be an invaluable source of inspiration for many writers of ghostly fiction. Although allegedly based on true events and thus not ghost stories in the strictest sense, the narrative form and presentation of Crowe's work, coupled with its significant influence on the genre, requires her inclusion here.

Selected bibliography

Light and Darkness, or, Mysteries of Life by Mrs Catherine Crowe, in Three Volumes. London: Henry Colburn, Publisher, 1850.

A collection of stories written as 'faction'. The source material used by Crowe for her story, *The Lycanthropist*, was also used by Guy Endore as the basis for his famous novel, *The Werewolf of Paris* (1933).

Ghosts and Family Legends: a Volume for Christmas by Mrs Crowe. London: Thomas Cautley Newby, Publisher, 1859.
A collection of 'faction' capitalising on the Victorian association of the ghost story with the Christmas season. The stories were related by the author's friends as they sat round the fire over eight consecutive evenings and are conversational in tone. The book also includes four letters received by the author which detail ghostly experiences.

The Night Side of Nature, or, Ghosts and Ghost Seers by Catherine Crowe, in Two Volumes. London: T.C. Newby, 1848.
Dreams, warnings, double-dreaming, doppelgängers, apparitions, haunted houses, and clairvoyance: this non-fiction work was Crowe's most popular book and it ran to many editions. It was highly influential in moulding the popular perception of ghostly phenomena for many years after its publication.

Spiritualism, and the Age We Live In by Catherine Crowe. London: T.C. Newby, Publisher, 1859.
A non-fiction exploration of popular spiritualism.

Lady Dilke (1840-1904)

An early feminist, Lady Emilia Francis Strong Dilke's main contribution to literature was in the field of cultural history, where she specialised in the art of eighteenth-century France.

Much of Dilke's fiction is pervaded by sentimental religiosity, a feature that particularly undermines the effectiveness of her supernatural work. Her ghost stories are commonly allegorical in nature and often pervaded by an unreal or dreamlike atmosphere that hampers their narrative pace and blunts horrific effects. A memoir of Dilke, written by her husband Sir Charles Dilke after her death, suggests that Lady Dilke often used her supernatural writing to purge her deepest personal fears.

Selected bibliography

The Shrine of Death and Other Stories by Lady Dilke. London: George Routledge & Sons, 1886.
A weak collection of fantasy, horror and supernatural tales written in a heavily romantic style. The work was produced in a limited edition of 150 copies.

The Book of the Spiritual Life by the Late Lady Dilke with a Memoir of the Author by the Rt. Hon. Sir Charles W. Dilke, with Portraits and Illustrations. London: John Murray, 1905.
Although most of this posthumous work is of a devotional nature, it also includes two supernatural short stories, The Mirror of the Soul *and* The Last Hour, *which together with some unfinished stories and sketches were to have formed the basis of Dilke's third short story collection.*

Amelia B. Edwards (1831-1892)

Together with Charlotte Riddell and Mrs Oliphant, Amelia Edwards is one of the foremost female ghost story writers of the Victorian period. Her work bridges the gap between the earlier Gothic style and the more sophisticated mid-Victorian ghost tradition made popular by authors such as Charles Dickens and Elizabeth Gaskell.

A prolific writer of popular novels, Edwards became fascinated by the world of Ancient Egypt following a visit to the country in 1873. She campaigned vigorously for the newly formed Egypt Exploration Society, lecturing regularly in Europe and America and publishing several popular works on the subject of Egyptian history.

Edwards' ghost stories are regarded by many critics as classics of the genre and are regularly reprinted in supernatural anthologies. This is arguably the best way to enjoy them, for if read sequentially one may experience a certain sense of *déjà vu* as similarities in their construction become increasingly apparent.

Edwards wrote her ghost stories chiefly for Christmas editions of popular magazines, including those of Charles Dickens, and several were published anonymously. It is therefore quite possible that some of her tales remain undiscovered due to their lack of attribution.

Edwards' supernatural work was collected by Richard Dalby as *The Phantom Coach* (1999) and published by the Canadian Ash-Tree Press in a limited edition of 500 copies.

Selected bibliography

Miss Carew by Amelia B. Edwards, in Three Volumes.

London: Hurst and Blackett, Publishers, Successors to Henry Colburn, 1865.

A linked series of stories, many of which are supernatural, often used by anthologists searching for classic examples of the Victorian ghost story. The North Mail *is perhaps better known under its more popular title,* The Phantom Coach; Number Three *has also been regularly reprinted as* How the Third Floor Knew the Potteries.

Monsieur Maurice: a New Novelette and Other Tales by Amelia B. Edwards in Three Volumes. London: Hurst and Blackett, Publishers, 1873.

A collection of tales ranging from the religious to the sentimental and including some of Edwards' best work. In addition to the title ghost novella, the collection contains the regularly anthologised tale The Engineer's Story *which is sometimes reprinted as* The Engineer.

Henrietta Dorothy Everett (1851-1923)
(Pseudonym: Theo Douglas)

Now largely forgotten, Henrietta Everett was a highly popular novelist during the period 1890-1920, often writing under the pseudonym of Theo Douglas. While most of the author's works have not aged particularly well, they are of interest as typical examples of late Victorian pulp fiction.

Everett's sole supernatural collection, *The Death-Mask and Other Ghosts*, was singled out for praise by M.R. James in his essay, *Some Remarks on Ghost Stories* (1929), but despite this, the tales have largely been ignored since the author's death and rarely anthologised.

More recently, however, her work has been rediscovered by a new generation of readers and collectors interested in classic ghost fiction who have found her unusual blend of horror and the supernatural to be of some interest.

Selected bibliography

The Death-Mask and Other Ghosts by Mrs H.D. Everett. London: Philip Allan & Co., 1920.
A fine collection of Victorian ghosts, the title tale being the author's most celebrated work in the genre. The collection was reprinted in a limited numbered edition by the Ghost Story Press (1995) with a new introduction by the anthologist Richard Dalby.

Violet Mary Firth (1890-1946)
(Pseudonym: Dion Fortune)

One of the most prominent occultists of her generation, Firth was originally a member of the infamous English magical society, the Golden Dawn, but left following the First World War to found her own group based on her theories of tantric yoga and white magic.

Firth wrote several books documenting her magical system which, unlike the works of many of her contemporaries, are still in print today.

Firth's fiction writing career began well with a series of short occult detective stories that combined her magical theories with strong plots and atmospheric settings. However, it was with a sequence of occult novels that the author really made her mark.

Like the works of her contemporary, Aleister Crowley, whose career shares some features with her own, Firth's novels contain thinly disguised portraits of prominent British occultists and their practices. Unfortunately, Firth's magical beliefs came to dominate her fiction, making it all but impenetrable to the ordinary reader – a situation exacerbated by increasingly flimsy plots. Despite this, her earlier supernatural tales can still be enjoyed.

Selected bibliography

The Secrets of Dr Taverner by Dion Fortune. London: Noel Douglas, 1926.
A well-paced collection of occult detective tales, although like many works in this sub-genre, some may find the concentration on occult theory heavy going.

The Demon Lover by Dion Fortune. London: Noel Douglas, 1927.
An occult thriller that pits a black magic group against devotees of tantric magic. A well-paced novel of sustained interest.

The Winged Bull: A Romance of Modern Magic by Dion Fortune. London: Williams & Norgate Ltd., 1935.
Far less commercial than the author's earlier work, this black magic novel begins a trend in her work of sacrificing coherent plots for abstract occultist speculation.

The Sea Priestess by Dion Fortune. London: Published by the Author, 1938.
A magical adventure featuring a somewhat idealised character,

'Vivian Le Fay Morgan'. The novel is heavily laced with occult symbolism and the author's theories of sex-magic.

Sane Occultism by Dion Fortune. London: Rider & Co., 1929.
A non-fiction work.

Spiritualism in the Light of Occult Science by Dion Fortune. London: Rider & Co., 1931.
A non-fiction work.

Practical Occultism in Daily Life by Dion Fortune. London: Williams & Norgate Ltd., 1935.
A non-fiction work.

Wilhelmina Fitzclarence, Countess of Munster (1830-1906)

Wilhemina Fitzclarence was something of a literary late starter, publishing her first book when she was nearly sixty years of age. Despite this, she still managed to write a series of successful novels over the next two decades as well as an autobiography. Her work includes the superlative collection, *Ghostly Tales* (1896).

Fitzclarence's ghost stories are usually more swiftly paced than those of her contemporaries and this, coupled with a plain and direct writing style, means the tales have retained their interest and bear re-examination by a new generation of readers.

Several have been revived in recent years by anthologists such as Hugh Lamb looking for powerful but less familiar supernatural material.

Selected bibliography

Ghostly Tales by the Countess of Munster. London: Hutchinson & Co., 1896.
A rare collection of high quality Victorian ghost stories, which seems several decades ahead of its time.

Lettice Galbraith (?-?)

Lettice Galbraith is a mysterious figure about whom little is known apart from the fact that she published a novel and two collections of short stories in 1893, followed by the ghost story, *The Blue Room*, in 1897. She is much admired among aficionados of ghostly fiction who believe her work ranks among that of leading writers in the genre.

Selected bibliography

The Blue Room and Other Ghost Stories by Lettice Galbraith. Wales: Sarob Press, 1999.
This collection of seven of Galbraith's tales is edited and introduced by Richard Dalby. It reprints six stories in Galbraith's collection, New Ghost Stories, *a sixpenny paperback published by Ward, Lock & Co in 1893. The volume also includes her ghost story,* The Blue Room, *which originally appeared in MacMillan's Magazine in 1897.*

The Shadow on the Blind and Other Stories by Louisa Baldwin and Lettice Galbraith. Hertfordshire: Wordsworth Editions, 2007.
This volume includes The Blue Room *and six other tales by Galbraith as well as ten short stories by Baldwin (See separate entry on this author).*

Mrs Gaskell (1810-1865)

Elizabeth Cleghorn Stevenson was born in London but following the early death of her mother was brought up in Knutsford, Cheshire, by an aunt. At the age of 21, she married William Gaskell, a Unitarian minister, and went to live with him in the industrial city of Manchester.

Encouraged by her husband, Gaskell began to write, at first in collaboration with him and later on her own. After several years of writing short magazine pieces, literary success came in 1848 with the publication of her novel, *Mary Barton*.

Charles Dickens was impressed by Gaskell's work, and invited her to contribute material to his popular magazine *Household Words*. Much of Gaskell's work, including the celebrated novel, *Cranford* (1853), made its first appearance in the magazine. During this period, Gaskell became friends with the writer Charlotte Brontë and later wrote a classic biography of her fellow novelist.

Gaskell's supernatural fiction ranks among the best of the Victorian period, with several of her most famous tales, including *The Old Nurse's Story* (1852) and *The Squire's Story* (1853), originally appearing in Christmas issues of *Household Words*. Gaskell's ghost tales are scattered throughout various periodicals and books of short stories and no single volume collection existed until 1978 when Michael Ashley produced *Mrs Gaskell's Tales of Mystery and Horror*.

Together with Dickens' work, Gaskell's ghost fiction

helped consolidate the association of the supernatural tale with the Victorian Christmas. Gaskell claimed to have seen a ghost and her belief in their reality may have added an extra dimension to her macabre writing. However, the main reason for her success is the combination of superb narrative technique and skilled control of atmosphere.

An additional reason for the popularity of Gaskell's supernatural work during the Victorian period is its lack of moral ambiguity. While some modern readers might find this moralistic standpoint a little simplistic, there is no doubting the effectiveness of Gaskell's writing. Most of her ghost stories are as enjoyable today as when they first appeared.

Selected bibliography

Round the Sofa by the Author of 'Mary Barton', 'Life of Charlotte Brontë', &c. &c., Two Volumes. London: Sampson Low, Son & Co., 1859.
A series of linked stories told in Margaret Dawson's sitting room in Edinburgh. The work includes The Doom of the Griffiths *which was Gaskell's first ghost story and* The Poor Clare, *about the effects of a curse.*

Right at Last and Other Tales by the Author of 'Mary Barton', 'Life of Charlotte Brontë', 'Round the Sofa' &c. London: Sampson Low, Son & Co., 1860.
The first book appearance of Lois the Witch *which had appeared in periodical form in* All the Year Round *during the previous year. An illustrated edition of Gaskell's short witchcraft novel was published in 1960 in London by Methuen, with pictures by Faith Jaques.*

The Grey Woman and Other Tales by Mrs Gaskell. London: Smith Elder & Co., 1865.
A mainstream collection of stories containing the supernatural tale, Curious if True.

Dora Havers (later Boulger) (1847-1923)
(Pseudonym: Theo Gift)

The popular author Dora Havers created her pseudonym, Theo Gift, for her one venture into the supernatural genre: a short story collection, *Not for the Night-Time* (1889).

A prolific writer of mainstream fiction, Havers was a regular contributor to Victorian magazines, including Charles Dickens' famous periodical *All the Year Round*. Havers also wrote several children's stories, collaborating on occasion with another writer of ghostly tales, E. Nesbit (author of *The Railway Children*, 1906), also featured in this volume.

Selected bibliography

Not for the Night-Time by Theo Gift. London: Roper & Drowley, 1889.
Apart from the much anthologised story, Dog or Demon?, *Havers' sole supernatural work is a rather pedestrian but highly regarded collection of mid-Victorian ghost stories. Although the author demonstrates an ability to convey moments of fear and is capable of solid plot development, most tales lack true originality. A limited edition of the work, edited and introduced by Richard Dalby, was published by the Welsh Sarob Press in 2000.*

Mary Elizabeth Hawker (1848-1908)
(Pseudonym: Lanoe Falconer)

Mary Hawker began writing professionally relatively late in life, publishing her first novella in 1890 at the age of forty-two. However, the success of her work encouraged her to continue until illness brought her literary career to a premature end.

While most of Hawker's work was romantic fiction, she did publish one item of interest to the ghost story enthusiast: the novel, *Cecilia de Noël* (1891).

Hawker's supernatural style did not differ markedly from that of her popular romances and *Cecilia de Noël* might be considered a successful variation on the author's more usual subject matter, although the work is slightly marred by over-sentimentality and class consciousness.

Selected bibliography

Cecilia de Noël by Lanoe Falconer. London and New York: Macmillan and Co., 1891.
A ghost novel of considerable subtlety and imagination. The plot examines different reactions to the same supernatural events from the viewpoint of several characters.

Clemence Annie Housman (1861-1955)

A sister of the artist and writer Laurence Housman and poet A.E. Housman, Clemence Housman had a short but impressive writing career at the end of the nineteenth century.

Her importance to the supernatural genre lies with a single novel, *The Were-Wolf* (1895), written for the amusement of her fellow art students while she and her brother Laurence were studying in London.

Although Clemence wrote several further works on completion of her studies, she devoted most of her energies to the cause of women's suffrage and in later years focused on using her graphic art skills to illustrate a number of Laurence's fantasy works.

The Were-Wolf (1896) is written in a rather heavy and consciously antique manner which parallels the author's favoured Pre-Raphaelite style of illustration.

The novel is highly allegorical in nature and pervaded by a strongly moralist tone, but in spite of this, it remains one of the most original and thought-provoking works of werewolf literature.

Selected bibliography

The Were-Wolf by Clemence Housman with Six Illustrations by Laurence Housman. London: John Lane at the Bodley Head; Chicago: Way and Williams, 1896.
One of the classic stories of lycanthropy. The work is illustrated by Clemence's brother.

The Unknown Sea by Clemence Housman. London: Duckworth and Co., 1898
A strange and atmospheric supernatural phantasy about a young man's love for a possibly vampiric sea witch.

Isobel Violet Hunt (1862-1942)

The daughter of a prominent artist of the Pre-Raphaelite group, Alfred W. Hunt, Violet Hunt became a well-known figure on London's literary scene during the first decades of the twentieth century.

An early feminist, Hunt's work offered a penetrating examination of Victorian morality and social convention and she experimented with various literary forms throughout her career to find the best way to express her then radical views.

Hunt knew many of the leading writers of the period, including Joseph Conrad, D.H. Lawrence and Henry James. James in particular was a significant influence on her writing, and her ghostly tales are reminiscent of his work and that of his fellow American, Edith Wharton.

Hunt shares their subtlety and careful crafting as well as the use of the supernatural to highlight the ironies and strangeness of everyday life. Her tales continue to stand the test of time.

Selected bibliography

Tales of the Uneasy by Violet Hunt. London: William Heinemann, 1911.
Hunt's first collection with supernatural content assembles revised versions of stories which had previously appeared in a variety of magazines. Although not all the stories are supernatural, those which are demonstrate a restraint and discipline which would have impressed even M.R. James.

More Tales of the Uneasy by Violet Hunt. London:
William Heinemann Ltd., 1925.

A slightly weaker collection than Tales of the Uneasy,
containing just four tales, two of which, Love's Last Leave *and*
The Night of No Weather *are ghostly. Hunt's fine sense of
irony is apparent throughout and the book includes a lengthy
preface by the author.*

Margaret Emma Faith Irwin (1889-1967)

Margaret Irwin was a leading historical novelist
between the two world wars and also wrote a
considerable number of short stories, several of which
were supernatural. Her tales were originally written for
publication in popular periodicals of the time, such as
the *London Mercury*, and later reprinted in one of her
numerous volumes of short stories.

Irwin's undoubted mastery of historical atmosphere
adds considerable authenticity to her early ghost
stories, while her accomplished handling of plot and
pace contribute greatly to their lasting success.

However, the high quality of Irwin's early work in the
genre was not sustained throughout her career, and
many of her later stories are considerably weaker.

More recently, Irwin's work has been rediscovered and
championed by feminist critics for their subtle
perception and depth of psychological insight.

Selected bibliography

Madame Fears the Dark: Seven Stories and a Play by

Margaret Irwin. London: Chatto & Windus, 1935.
A rare and sought after collection of highly original short stories. While some tales might be considered fantasy rather than supernatural fiction, several included in this collection represent the best of Irwin's early ghostly work.

Still She Wished for Company by Margaret Irwin. London: William Heinemann Ltd., 1924.
An unusual supernatural novel in which characters from both past and future encounter each other as 'ghosts'. An original and well-paced piece of work.

Jessie Douglas Kerruish (1884-1949)

Jessie Kerruish is best known today for her historical works, both fiction and non-fiction. She began her literary career by contributing stories and articles to a number of popular magazines and went on to produce a series of well-received historical novels.

Although some of Kerruish's short stories fall into the ghostly category, it is her third novel, *The Undying Monster* (1922), that is of greatest significance to the supernatural genre. This story of lycanthropy, while sometimes overburdened with occult jargon, still retains much of its original power and continues to reward the modern reader in search of lesser-known macabre tales.

Kerruish contributed several tales to her friend Christine Campbell Thompson's *Not at Night* series of supernatural anthologies, but failing health brought her writing career to a premature end.

Selected bibliography

The Undying Monster: A Tale of the Fifth Dimension by Jessie Douglas Kerruish. London: Heath Cranton Limited, 1922.
Kerruish's supernatural masterpiece is one of a select group of classic werewolf novels and features a rare example of a female occult detective, Luna Bartendale. The book was filmed in 1942.

Margery Lawrence (1889-1969)

Margery Lawrence was born in Wolverhampton and studied art before she decided on a writing career. Her first work, a volume of poetry, was published in 1913, and by the end of the First World War she had begun to concentrate on writing novels. A prolific writer of romantic and adventure fiction, Lawrence also worked as a journalist, and wrote several non-fiction works together with numerous short stories.

Her interest in the supernatural led her to become an ardent spiritualist in later life, and much of her fiction reflects her belief in the reality of occult phenomena. Lawrence claimed to be in touch with the spirits of dead relatives and wrote several works championing the spiritualist cause.

She also joined The Ghost Club (still in existence today), a society dedicated to the investigation of ghostly phenomena, and sometimes used the supernatural experiences of fellow members as material for her fiction.

While sometimes hampered by a verbose and jargon-laden style, Lawrence's ghost fiction is notable for its sophisticated execution and range of subject matter. Her Miles Pennoyer occult detective stories are among the best in this sub-genre and rank with those of masters such as Algernon Blackwood and William Hope Hodgson. Considering her beliefs, it is perhaps surprising that Lawrence's ghosts are frequently portrayed as horrific and vengeful spirits rather than the lost souls common to spiritualist fiction.

Although Lawrence's later occult novels were quite popular during her lifetime, her work has been largely ignored since her death and rarely reprinted. However, the anthologist Richard Dalby has assisted in a re-evaluation of her work by the inclusion of her short stories in several of his supernatural fiction anthologies.

Selected bibliography

Nights of the Round Table: a Book of Strange Tales Recorded by Margery H. Lawrence. London: Hutchinson & Co. (Publishers), Ltd., 1926.
A collection of short stories presented as a series of supposedly true tales related by the guests at a monthly dinner party. How Pan Delivered Little Ingleton *has also been reprinted under the title Mr* Minchin's Midsummer. *The work was reprinted in 1998 by the Canadian Ash-Tree Press with an introduction by Richard Dalby, in a limited edition of 500 copies.*

The Terraces of Night: (Being Further Chronicles of The Club of the Round Table) by Margery Lawrence. London: Hurst & Blackett Ltd., 1932.
A fine collection of macabre short stories. Mare Amore *has also appeared under the title* Storm. *The work was reprinted in 1999 by the Canadian Ash-Tree Press with an informative new*

introduction by Richard Dalby, in a limited edition of 600 copies.

Number Seven Queer Street: Being Some Stories Taken From the Private Casebook of Dr Miles Pennoyer, Recorded by his Friend & Occasional Assistant Jerome Latimer by Margery Lawrence. London: Robert Hale Limited, 1945.
A high quality collection of occult detective tales involving the supernatural sleuth, Miles Pennoyer. As with some other examples of the occult detective sub-genre, the success of some stories is compromised by the author's use of obscure occult jargon.

The Bridge of Wonder by Margery Lawrence. London: Robert Hale Limited, 1939.
A large-scale spiritualist novel which, although highly popular in its time, is now somewhat dated in style.

The Rent in the Veil by Margery Lawrence. London: Robert Hale Limited, 1951.
A reincarnationist romance that explores the power of love over death. While the work contains some effective scenes it is a somewhat over-extended piece.

Bride of Darkness by Margery Lawrence. London: Robert Hale, 1967.
An uneven supernatural romance about a man's marriage to a witch.

Ferry over Jordan by Margery Lawrence. London: Robert Hale Limited, 1944.
Lawrence's most interesting and commercially successful non-fiction spiritualist work.

Helen Magdalene Leys (1892-1965)
(Pseudonym: Eleanor Scott)

After a considerable period of neglect, Leys' supernatural works are now being rediscovered by a new generation of anthologists and readers.

Leys wrote several popular mainstream novels between the two world wars, but her most effective work is undoubtedly the ghost story collection, *Randalls Round* (1929).

While several of the author's tales, including the masterful *Celui-là*, have been compared to the work of M.R. James, Leys' stories have a unique and powerful character of their own. The original and varied nature of these fine but disturbing tales may be due in part to their origin, since according to Leys, all were suggested by her dreams.

Leys wrote: 'These dreams, as I say, were terrifying to the dreamer. I know what young Grindley endured in *The Room* because I myself have suffered the experience in a dream.'

The anthologist and bibliographer Richard Dalby managed to piece together the few known facts about this mysterious author in an article for issue 17 of the magazine, *Ghosts and Scholars*.

Selected bibliography

Sheaves from the Cornhill. London: John Murray, 1926.
This collection of items from The Cornhill Magazine, *selected*

by its editor, Leonard Huxley, includes the first appearance of Scott's supernatural tale, The Room. *The story is attributed to 'H.M. Leys'.*

Randalls Round by Eleanor Scott. London: Ernest Benn Limited, 1929.
A rare and highly regarded collection of original ghostly tales. It was republished in 1996 in a limited edition of 500 copies by the Ash-Tree Press, with a new introduction by Richard Dalby.

Dorothy Macardle (1889-1958)

Together with her friends, W.B. Yeats and George Russell, Dorothy Macardle was a prominent figure in Irish literary society during the early years of the twentieth century.

An author, historian and ardent Irish republican, Macardle's first ghost stories were written during her imprisonment in 1922 for nationalist activities; possibly because of its unhappy associations, she did not to return to the genre for nearly twenty years.

Macardle's early stories were written for magazine publication and their delicate atmosphere and traditional Irish backgrounds are typical of the 'Celtic twilight' school of literature.

During her later years, Macardle wrote a series of genre novels which successfully integrated supernatural themes and motifs within the framework of a mainstream thriller.

Her early short stories have a period charm but

relatively weak plots, while the later novels are more polished in style but less original.

Selected bibliography

Dark Enchantment by Dorothy Macardle. London: Peter Davies, 1953.
A story of magic set in the French Alps which is slightly reminiscent of Algernon Blackwood's tale Ancient Sorceries, *although rather less successfully executed.*

Uneasy Freehold by Dorothy Macardle. London: Peter Davies, 1941.
A superior, if conventional, haunted house novel which is somewhat marred by an over-sentimental treatment. The work was published in the USA as The Uninvited *and achieved bestseller status. It was later filmed under its American title.*

Fantastic Summer by Dorothy Macardle. London: Peter Davies, 1946.
A supernatural thriller about psychic powers that partly recaptures the subtle atmosphere of the author's early stories. The work was published in the USA as The Unforeseen.

Mary Mackay (1855-1924)
(Pseudonym: Marie Corelli)

Mary Mackay adopted the stage name Marie Corelli early in life while working as a musician. She experienced some success in her musical career, but left the profession when a psychic experience prompted her to begin a study of spiritualism and the occult.

Mackay managed to communicate her spiritualist insights within the framework of commercial romantic fiction and created a highly successful series of hybrid novels beginning with *A Romance of Two Worlds* (1886) and including science fiction fantasies such as *The Secret Power* (1921).

Mackay eventually became Britain's most commercially successful novelist of the period, developing a wide readership in America and including Queen Victoria among her admirers.

In her long career, Mackay produced nearly thirty books, many of which have some supernatural content.

Despite popular acclaim however, Mackay expressed annoyance that her work did not receive the serious critical approval she felt it deserved and increasingly believed the literary establishment had formed a conspiracy against her. Her beliefs became even more extreme in later years as her popularity began to diminish and she came to believe she was the reincarnation of William Shakespeare.

Mackay's supernatural fiction shares the verbosity and sentimentality of much of her other work. While she is capable of original story ideas, these are often spoilt by poor characterisation and plotting.

Despite their huge contemporary popularity, Mackay's stories are chiefly of interest today for their effect on popular beliefs about the supernatural during the late Victorian and Edwardian eras and their influence on other writers in the genre.

Selected bibliography

A Romance of Two Worlds: A Novel by Marie Corelli, in Two Volumes. London: Richard Bentley and Son, 1886.
A strange occult novel involving interplanetary travel in search of spiritual development. Highly popular at the time of publication but now rather dated.

The Soul of Lilith by Marie Corelli, in Three Volumes. London: Richard Bentley and Son, 1892.
An average quality supernatural fantasy involving Arabian magic.

The Strange Visitation of Josiah McNason: a Christmas Ghost Story by Marie Corelli; Illustrated by H. R. Millar. London: George Newnes, 1904.
A reworking of Dickens' A Christmas Carol. *A companion to the Christmas number of the* Strand Magazine *for 1904.*

Florence Marryat (1838-1899)

Florence Marryat was the daughter of another occasional writer of supernatural tales, Captain Frederick Marryat. In addition to bringing up eight children from her first marriage, she worked at various times as an actress, singer, and head of a school of journalism.

Her literary reputation grew from her successful series of novels about fashionable society life in London. Much of her background material was gained through her work as editor of *London Society Magazine*. In her later years, Marryat managed to reconcile her

Catholicism with a deep interest in spiritualism and wrote several works on the subject.

Marryat's shorter supernatural work is scattered throughout her more general collections and originally appeared in periodical form, most frequently *Temple Bar*.

A competent commercial writer, Marryat's ghostly fiction is well-constructed if somewhat unoriginal and includes most of the standard props found in the genre since the Gothic period.

Unlike many of her contemporaries, however, much of Marryat's work is still enjoyable and would be of interest to any lover of the traditional Victorian ghost story.

Selected bibliography

A Moment of Madness, and Other Stories by Florence Marryat, in Three Volumes. London: F. V. White & Co., 1883.
A general collection of Marryat's short stories reprinted from Temple Bar *magazine. Includes several ghost stories which were also published in the same year by Tauchnitz in Leipzig under the title,* The Ghost of Charlotte Cray.

The Strange Transfiguration of Hannah Stubbs by Florence Marryat. London: Hutchinson and Co., 1896.
One of the earliest novels to tackle the subject of spirit possession. An original subject competently tackled.

The Blood of the Vampire by Florence Marryat. London: Hutchinson & Co., 1897.

Written in the same year as Bram Stoker's Dracula, *this novel is a complex fin de siècle tale of inherited psychic vampirism with touches of voodoo, spiritualism and humour.*

There is no Death by Florence Marryat. London: Kegan Paul, Trench, Trübner & Co., Ltd, 1891.
A non-fiction account of the author's various spiritualist investigations, including descriptions of the activities of several popular mediums.

The Spirit World by Florence Marryat. London: F. V. White & Co., 1894.
An account of the author's later spiritualist experiences, including a chapter on 'how to investigate spiritualism'.

Flora Macdonald Mayor (1872-1932)

Born into a wealthy family at the height of the Victorian era, Flora Macdonald Mayor rejected her conventional middle class upbringing for a career on the stage.

However, experience of theatrical life convinced her that her future lay elsewhere.

Mayor originally used her writing as a form of emotional release after the tragic death of her fiancé in India. The high quality of her work was readily acknowledged by her literary contemporaries, including the poet John Masefield who wrote a preface to her acclaimed novel, *The Third Miss Symons* (1913).

Mayor's legacy was increasingly ignored following her death in 1932, although she was rediscovered by a new generation of readers thanks to Virago Press which republished several of her carefully crafted novels of rural life.

Mayor's ghost stories were admired by the genre's master writer, M.R. James, and few modern readers would disagree with his evaluation. Not only do her tales exhibit a fine control of atmosphere, but they regularly include highly original plot twists and unusually rounded characterisation.

Mayor manages to successfully combine the best of the English ghost tradition with elements of her own unique style, and her writing should appeal to anyone interested in supernatural fiction.

Selected bibliography

The Room Opposite and Other Tales of Mystery and Imagination by F. M. Mayor. London: Longmans, Green and Co., 1935.
A posthumous collection of miscellaneous short stories, including some highly effective ghostly tales.

Mrs Molesworth (1839-1921)

Although born in Holland, Mary Louisa Stewart Molesworth spent most of her long life in Britain.

She was a prolific author of over one hundred children's books, several of which have remained in print to the present day as minor classics of children's literature.

In addition, Molesworth wrote a small number of high quality ghostly works which have also stood the test of time. One reason for her enduring popularity, in comparison to many of her contemporaries, is her early adoption of a more modern and straightforward writing style. Molesworth deftly avoids the overblown excesses of much Victorian pulp prose, telling her tales in a manner that retains and rewards a reader's interest in her often complex plots.

The appeal and effectiveness of Molesworth's stories are further enhanced by her skilful use of humour as a contrast to the more disturbing scenes of supernatural horror.

Selected bibliography

Uncanny Tales by Mrs Molesworth. London: Hutchinson & Co., 1896.
Molesworth's best collection of supernatural and fantasy tales. The Shadow in the Moonlight *is generally acknowledged to be a minor masterpiece of the ghost story genre.*

The Wrong Envelope and Other Stories by Mrs Molesworth. London: Macmillan and Co. Limited; New York: The Macmillan Company, 1906.
A general collection that includes Molesworth's ghost story, A Strange Messenger, *together with the tale,* A Ghost of the Pampas *by the author's son, Bevil.*

Rosa Mulholland 1841-1921
(Lady Gilbert)

A frequent contributor to Charles Dickens' popular *All*

the Year Round magazine, the versatile Rosa Mulholland wrote several successful works of biography and children's fiction and a small number of supernatural works. The latter include short stories, often commissioned especially for the celebrated Christmas issues of *All the Year Round*, and novels incorporating elements of folklore from Mulholland's native Ireland.

The author's homeland also provided both setting and subject matter for her more mainstream work, much of which chronicles the lives of the Irish rural poor.

Selected bibliography

The Haunted Organist of Hurly Burly and Other Stories by Rosa Mulholland. London: Hutchinson and Co., 1891.
A general collection containing several good quality supernatural tales.

Banshee Castle by Rosa Mulholland, with Twelve Full-Page Illustrations by John H. Bacon. London, Glasgow and Dublin: Blackie & Son Limited, 1895.
A popular mainstream novel containing both ghostly and Gothic features. The book was later republished in 1925 under the title, The Girls of Banshee Castle.

Dinah Maria Mulock 1826-1887
(Also known as Mrs Craik)

Dinah Mulock enjoyed a highly successful and diverse writing career and is perhaps best known today for her novel, *John Halifax, Gentleman* (1857). A prolific author of fiction, essays and poetry, Mulock contributed many items, including some supernatural material, to the popular magazines of the mid-Victorian period.

Although she draws on familiar settings for her stories, Mulock breathes fresh life into the well-worn haunted house tale with a style and skill very much her own. In addition to her traditional ghost stories, Mulock wrote a book of fairy tales, *Is it True?* (1872), based on folk tales and legends.

Like most of her more mainstream work, Mulock's supernatural fiction has been largely neglected since her death. However, some of her ghost stories have appeared in more recent anthologies. Mulock's tales certainly deserve rediscovery as several are examples of the Victorian ghost tradition at its very best.

Selected bibliography

Avillion and Other Tales by the Author of 'Olive', 'The Head of the Family', 'Agatha's Husband', &c. &c, in Three Volumes. London: Smith, Elder and Co.; Bombay: Smith, Taylor and Co., 1853.
A general collection of tales, including the unusual supernatural tale, The Rosicrucian, *the story of a young man's encounter with an ancient spirit of fire.*

Nothing New: Tales by the Author of 'John Halifax, Gentleman', &c. &c., in Two Volumes. London: Hurst and Blackett Publishers, Successors to Henry Colburn, 1857.
A collection of miscellaneous tales, including the classic ghost story, The last House in C---- Street.

E. Nesbit (1858-1924)

Edith Nesbit was born in Kennington and educated in both England and continental Europe. Although she contributed poetry to magazines while still in her teens she did not write professionally until forced to by the collapse of her husband's business in 1880. The emotional strain of this period is detectable in her early fiction, much of which includes elements of horror or the supernatural.

Despite their domestic difficulties, Nesbit and her husband found time to assist in the foundation of the Fabian Society, a cause which introduced them to many of the foremost socialist writers of the time, including Bernard Shaw and H.G. Wells.

Although Nesbit's contributions to magazines helped stabilise family finances, literary recognition did not come until the publication of her children's novel, *The Adventure of the Shell Seekers* (1899). A series of classic children's novels followed, including *Five Children and It* (1902), *The Phoenix and the Carpet* (1904) and *The Railway Children* (1906).

Their success gave Nesbit a much needed period of financial stability, during which she raised her rather unconventional family which included both her own children and those of her husband's mistress.

Nesbit's husband died in 1914 and after three difficult years of illness and financial uncertainty, she married an old family friend, Thomas Terry Tucker. The author's second marriage was happier than her first and lasted until her death seven years later in 1924.

Nesbit's macabre stories vary significantly in quality and have been criticised for wooden characterisation, crude construction and occasionally contrived plots. This is perhaps understandable as much of Nesbit's supernatural fiction dates from the early and most pressured period of her writing career.

However, among the author's prolific if rather uneven output are a number of excellent ghost stories which display her considerable psychological insight and originality. Often, Nesbit's most compelling stories are based on incidents from her childhood, during which she claimed to have lived in at least two haunted houses.

Although Nesbit eventually developed a deep interest in psychic matters, she did not compromise the quality of her writing by using the occult jargon so often adopted by writers wishing to demonstrate their supposed mystical erudition.

Nesbit's stories often flout both the moral and ghostly conventions of their time and deliver a higher level of horror than the work of most contemporaries.

When considering her unconventional and troubled domestic life, it is perhaps not too surprising that several of her supernatural tales deal with complex relationships between men and women and convey more than a hint of suppressed sexuality.

Nesbit's ghost and horror stories were largely neglected until their rediscovery by the anthologist Hugh Lamb who assembled two fine collections of

Nesbit's best work, *In the Dark* (1988) and *E. Nesbit's Tales of Terror* (1983).

Selected bibliography

Grim Tales by E. Nesbit. London: A. D. Innes & Co., 1893.
Nesbit's best collection of supernatural writing includes the regularly anthologised story, Man-Size in Marble.

Fear by E. Nesbit. London: Stanley Paul & Co., 1910.
A selection of the best of Nesbit's previously published supernatural tales together with some new material. The Shadow *has also been anthologised as* The Portent of the Shadow.

Dormant by E. Nesbit. London: Methuen & Co. Ltd., 1911.
A strange hybrid novel about the search for eternal youth by occult and scientific means which is closer to Nesbit's children's fantasies than her normal style of ghost fiction.

Mrs Oliphant (1828-1897)

Born in East Lothian, Margaret Oliphant Wilson Oliphant originally intended to pursue a career as a painter but decided instead to concentrate on writing. Her first novel, *Margaret Maitland* (1849), was well received and marked the start of a decade of literary success.

However, the premature death of her husband in 1859, and then her brother, left her with two families to support and substantial debts to repay. In response,

Oliphant increased her output while attempting to maintain her high literary standards and eventually produced over 130 novels and non-fiction works as well as numerous magazine pieces.

As might be expected, Oliphant's work varies significantly in quality reflecting the pressures she was under. Nevertheless, despite being dogged by ill health in later life, she wrote a substantial amount of high-quality work in several genres, including the supernatural. It is clear that she was an author of considerable talent and that without her financial worries she may have become one of the era's foremost writers.

Oliphant began contributing ghost stories to magazines in 1857, although her first hard cover collection, *Stories of the Seen and Unseen*, was not published until much later.

While several of her short stories are now counted among classics of the genre, her supernatural novels are significantly less successful due to heavy-handed moralising and an over-sentimental approach.

Since much of Oliphant's work was published anonymously, it is possible that a number of her supernatural stories still remain to be rediscovered within the pages of the magazines of the period.

Selected bibliography

Stories of the Seen and the Unseen by Mrs Oliphant. Edinburgh and London: William Blackwood and Sons, 1902.

A posthumous collection that includes the best of Oliphant's ghostly works.

The Wizard's Son: A Novel by Mrs Oliphant, in Three Volumes. London: Macmillan and Co., 1884.
An over-long novel about demonic possession set in an ancient Scottish castle.

Violet Paget (1856-1935)
(Pseudonym: Vernon Lee)

Violet Paget was born in the French town of Boulogne to a Welsh mother and a father descended from the French nobility. The family travelled around Europe for several years before settling in the Italian city of Florence. Despite her British citizenship, Paget did not visit England until 1881 and never chose to settle there.

Under the pseudonym of Vernon Lee she developed a considerable reputation as a cultural historian of her adopted country of Italy, first attracting critical attention with her work, *Studies in Eighteenth Century Italy* (1880).

From this point, she wrote a steady stream of essays, criticism and fiction, chiefly about the history, art and literature of post-medieval Italy. Her lush descriptions of renaissance and baroque culture in Florence and Rome appealed greatly to members of the aesthetic movement and were well suited to the spirit of *fin-de-siècle* decadence fashionable during the 1890s.

Although Paget wrote relatively few supernatural short stories, their quality gained her the respect of several connoisseurs of the genre, including M.R. James and Montague Summers*.

Not only do Paget's works have a psychological depth and subtlety rarely found in the genre, they also benefit from her detailed knowledge of Italian history and are packed with fascinating background detail.

It is difficult to generalise about Paget's ghostly fiction since it is highly diverse in both theme and setting. However, common motifs include the enduring power of evil and the illusory nature of time. Her stories also benefit greatly from her judicious use of humour and considerable writing technique.

Several reprint collections of Paget's macabre stories have been published under a variety of titles, including: *Supernatural Tales* (1955), *The Virgin of the Seven Daggers* (1962) and *Ravenna and Her Ghosts (1962)*.

Montague Summers (1880-1948) was an eccentric figure who wrote on the Gothic fiction genre, as well as producing works about witches, werewolves and vampires.

Selected bibliography

Hauntings: Fantastic Stories by Vernon Lee. London: William Heinemann, 1890.
An excellent collection of supernatural tales. The volume contains the ghostly novella, A Phantom Lover, *here given the title,* Oke of Okehurst.

Pope Jacynth and Other Fantastic Tales by Vernon Lee. London: Grant Richards, 1904.
A superior collection of varied and original ghostly tales. The

volume was later reprinted as a Corgi paperback under the title Ravenna and Her Ghosts (1962).

For Maurice: Five Unlikely Stories by Vernon Lee. London: John Lane, The Bodley Head Limited, 1927.
The author's final supernatural collection assembles tales from her early career and is of extremely high quality throughout. The book is dedicated to another occasional writer of weird tales, Maurice Baring. Winthrop's Adventure *has also appeared in supernatural fiction anthologies as* A Cultured Ghost.

A Phantom Lover: A Fantastic Story by Vernon Lee. Edinburgh and London: William Blackwood and Sons, 1886.
A well-written short supernatural novel of great subtlety and some ambiguity, displaying a fine control of ghostly atmosphere. The story was also included in E.F. Bleiler's 1971 collection, Five Victorian Ghost Novels.

Edith Pargeter (1913-1995)
(Pseudonym: Ellis Peters)

During a long literary career, Edith Pargeter wrote several moderately successful series of historical novels. However, it was under the pseudonym of Ellis Peters that she finally achieved cult status as the creator of the popular medieval sleuth, Brother Cadfael.

Pargeter was a prolific author and her historical works are meticulously researched period recreations. However, only one of the author's two supernatural novels makes significant use of her considerable historical expertise.

It is also notable that Pargeter's ghost novels are closer in style to the nineteenth century Gothic tradition than the contemporary antiquarian school of writers such as M.R. James, A.N.L. Munby or R.H. Malden.

Selected bibliography

The City Lies Four-Square: A Novel by Edith Pargeter. London: William Heinemann Limited, 1939.
A rather sentimental haunted house novel about a young doctor's efforts to assist a long-dead former inhabitant of his house to move on to the next world.

By Firelight by Edith Pargeter. London: William Heinemann Ltd., 1948.
Over-sentimentality hampers the supernatural effect in a love story which has parallels over three centuries. While both atmosphere and period are cleverly evoked, they are not successfully sustained. The work was published in America as By This Strange Fire.

Kate O'Brien Prichard and Hesketh Vernon Prichard
(Pseudonyms: E. and H. Heron)

Kate Prichard (1851-1935) brought her son Hesketh (1876-1922) back to England from India following the death of her husband, and the pair travelled widely in the following years.

In addition to writing several books, some in collaboration with his mother, Hesketh was at various times a big game hunter, soldier, county cricketer and explorer. His good looks and exceptional height of six foot six inches made him a striking figure.

Hesketh fought on the Western Front in World War One, where he commanded a corps of 'sharpshooters'. He later wrote what came to be regarded as the definitive textbook on the subject of sniping. Injuries sustained during the war made him a semi-invalid for much of the rest of his life.

The Prichards' main contribution to the supernatural genre is a series of stories they co-wrote about a psychic detective, Flaxman Low, which were published in *Pearsons Magazine* from January 1898 under the pseudonym, E. and H. Heron.

The description of the works as 'real' ghost stories caused some initial confusion, although their fictional nature was soon revealed. The Flaxman Low tales take a scientific approach to the supernatural, unusual for the time, reflecting the authors' belief that the subject would eventually succumb to rational explanation.

The tales were admired by many, including Arthur Conan Doyle and M.R. James, and are important examples in the development of the occult detective sub-genre. A further series was commissioned by *Pearsons*, who published a hardback edition of the tales under the authors' real names soon after their magazine publication.

Selected bibliography

Ghosts: Being the Experiences of Flaxman Low by K. and Hesketh Prichard (E. and H. Heron) with Twelve Illustrations by B.E. Minns. London: C. Arthur

Pearson: 1899.

This rare first edition of the collected magazine stories contains only twelve of the original seventy-two illustrations. An inferior partial reprint of Ghosts *without illustrations was published by Pearson in 1916. A facsimile reprint of the original magazine versions of the stories with all the original illustrations and an informative new introduction was published in a limited edition of 200 copies by the Ghost Story Press in 1993 as* Flaxman Low, Psychic Detective.

Gertrude M. Reynolds (1875-1939)
(Mrs Baillie Reynolds)

Although Gertrude Reynolds was a highly popular author of romantic novels and short stories during the period 1895-1935, she is largely unknown today. The style of romantic fiction that made her reputation has not aged well and now seems dated even to modern enthusiasts of the historical branch of the genre.

Reynolds' supernatural novels and short stories have matured more successfully and range from traditional ghost fiction to more sophisticated occult adventures. Readers looking for unfamiliar but well-crafted examples of the nineteenth century ghost tradition may be pleasantly surprised by a re-examination of Reynolds' supernatural work.

Selected bibliography

The Relations and What They Related: A Series of Weird Stories by Mrs Baillie Reynolds (G. M. Robins), with 16 Illustrations by A. D. McCormick. London: Hutchinson & Co., 1902.

This is Reynolds' best collection, consisting of a linked series of macabre stories told within the framework of a fictional family gathering.

A Castle to Let by Mrs Baillie Reynolds. London: Cassell and Company Ltd., 1917.
A romantic adventure with supernatural touches featuring a staple of the Gothic novel, the haunted castle. A well-written, if somewhat unconventional piece.

The Spell of Sarnia by Mrs Baillie Reynolds. London: Hodder and Stoughton Limited, 1925.
One of Reynolds' best works, the novel is an original occult thriller set in the Channel Islands.

Mrs J. H. Riddell (1832-1906)
(Pseudonyms include: Rainey Hawthorne; R.V. Sparling; F. G. Trafford)

Charlotte Cowen, later Mrs Riddell, was born in Carrickfergus, County Antrim, into a relatively wealthy Anglo-Irish family. However, her father died during her youth following financial ruin and Cowen moved with her mother to London, turning to writing to earn a living.

Cowen's mother did not live to see her daughter's remarkable success as a novelist, which began with the publication of her first book, *Zuriel's Grandchild* (1856). Shortly after her mother's death, Cowen married Joseph Riddell, a businessman with a rather mercurial personality.

Riddell based her most successful novels on her

husband's detailed knowledge of London business life and gained a considerable reputation as a popular quality writer during the mid-Victorian period.

In addition to her novels, Riddell contributed works to numerous magazines and Christmas annuals. However, as these were written under several pseudonyms or published anonymously, a complete bibliography of her work is problematic. Riddell also became editor and co-proprietor of *St James's Magazine*.

It is likely that Riddell's reputation as a mainstream novelist would have been greater if commercial pressures had not compelled her to increasingly sensationalise her fiction to satisfy her public.

In later life, as Riddell's popularity began to wane, she was further burdened by debts left by her husband following his death which she felt compelled to repay as a matter of honour. She eventually achieved this, but was then struck down by the illness which led to her death in 1906.

Riddell is acknowledged by connoisseurs as one of the greatest writers of supernatural fiction of the Victorian era and is particularly notable for creating ghost novels of sustained quality that remain of interest to this day.

The author's ghost stories, which regularly draw on the folklore of her native Ireland, are particularly remarkable for their depth of characterisation and attention to background detail.

Unlike most of her contemporaries, Riddell managed

to inject firm moral messages without resorting to sentimentality or artifice, her ghosts often acting as agents of retribution to redress past wrongs. Together with Charles Dickens and Sheridan Le Fanu, Riddell helped to define the classic Victorian ghost story, but has not yet received the wider recognition she so thoroughly deserves.

Selected bibliography

Weird Stories by Mrs J.H. Riddell. London: J. Hogg, 1882.
A seminal collection of Victorian ghost stories containing the much anthologised The Open Door. *A reprint edition with an introduction by the ghost story anthologist Herbert Van Thal was published by Home & Van Thal in 1946.*

The Collected Ghost Stories of Mrs J.H. Riddell Selected and introduced by E.F. Bleiler. New York: Dover Publications, Inc.; London: Constable and Company Ltd., c1977.
A useful collection of Riddell's short ghostly fiction, including the first UK book appearance of A Strange Christmas Game, *which has also been attributed to George A. Lawrence.*

Fairy Water: A Christmas Story by Mrs J.H. Riddell. London: George Routledge and Sons, 1873.
A high quality example of the Victorian ghost novel which has also been reprinted as The Haunted House at Latchford.

The Uninhabited House by Mrs J.H. Riddell. London: George Routledge and Sons, 1875.
Excellent supernatural novel, later included in E.F. Bleiler's Five Victorian Ghost Novels *(New York: Dover, 1971). The work was also reprinted as* The Haunted House at

Latchford *in Bleiler's* Three Supernatural Novels of the Victorian Period *(New York: Dover, 1975).*

The Haunted River: A Christmas Story by Mrs J.H. Riddell. London: George Routledge and Sons, 1877.
A first class example of the Victorian ghost novel.

The Disappearance of Mr. Jeremiah Redworth by Mrs J.H. Riddell. London: George Routledge and Sons, 1878.
An excellent supernatural novel and the last of Riddell's highly successful series of contributions to Routledge's Christmas Annual.

May Sinclair (1863-1946)
(Pseudonym: Julian Sinclair)

May Sinclair began writing professionally in her thirties and rapidly achieved great popularity as an author of novels and short stories of considerable psychological insight and originality.

Sinclair was an early follower of Freud and regularly incorporated elements of his theories in both her genre and more mainstream work. Later in her career she became a pioneer of the new 'stream of consciousness' style of writing and used the technique to great effect in her work.

A committed suffragette, Sinclair often used her position as a popular author to champion women's rights, as well as social and moral reform.

A firm spiritualist belief informs Sinclair's ghost

stories, and some modern readers might find them a trifle didactic due to the unquestioning nature of her faith. Despite this, the tales are well-crafted works of considerable depth and ingenuity and many scenes remain firmly lodged in the memory long after the final paragraph is read.

Selected bibliography

Uncanny Stories by May Sinclair; Illustrations by Jean de Bosschère. London: Hutchinson & Co., 1923.
A rare collection of psychological ghost stories of great subtlety and originality. The Flaw in the Crystal (1912) marked Sinclair's supernatural fiction début in the literary magazine, The English Review.

The Ghost Book: Sixteen New Stories of the Uncanny Compiled by Lady Cynthia Asquith. London: Hutchinson and Co. (Publishers) Ltd., 1926.
This volume includes the first appearance of Sinclair's tale, The Villa Désirée.

The Intercessor, and Other Stories by May Sinclair. London: Hutchinson & Co. (Publishers) Limited, 1931.
A collection of high-quality short stories, including several ghostly items with a psychological dimension. The supernatural title story was later filmed for television.

Eleanor Smith (1902-1945)

The daughter of the Earl of Birkenhead, Lady Eleanor Furneaux Smith claimed her ancestors included both aristocrats and gypsies. This belief resulted in her lifelong interest in Romany life and eventually led her to attempt to emulate the wandering gypsy lifestyle by joining a circus for a time.

Smith began her literary career during the inter-war years as a journalist, contributing newspaper society columns that chronicled the exploits of her upper-class friends.

From this modest beginning, she progressed to writing short stories and eventually novels, often based on her twin interests in gypsy culture and the theatre.

Her work proved popular in both Britain and America, and one of her historical novels, *The Man in Grey* (1941), was filmed in 1943.

A representative selection of Smith's supernatural work can be found in *Satan's Circus* (1931), a volume of unusual and polished tales made all the more convincing by their wealth of authentic background detail.

Selected bibliography

Satan's Circus and Other Stories by Eleanor Smith. London: Victor Gollancz Ltd., 1932.
A rare collection of macabre short stories on Smith's favourite subjects of the circus and gypsy life. The American edition of the work contains an additional supernatural tale, Whittington's Cat.

Lovers' Meeting by Eleanor Smith. London and Melbourne: Hutchinson & Co. (Publishers) Ltd., 1940.
A well-written but borderline supernatural romance with a

convincing historical background and unusual combination of magic, reincarnation and time travel.

Bessie Kyffin Taylor (d.1922)

Bessie Kyffin Taylor published her sole volume of ghost stories, *From Out of the Silence*, in 1920. This work, together with an earlier short non-supernatural piece, *Rosemary: a Duologue* (1918), seem to have been her only published books.

Although *From Out of the Silence* is packed with ghosts and supernatural events, it is a rather flawed collection. While the stories often begin with interesting and original touches, they rarely live up to their initial promise due to their competent but derivative treatment and lack of plot development.

Selected bibliography

From Out of the Silence: Seven Strange Stories by Bessie Kyffin-Taylor. London: Books Limited, 1920.
An average collection of stories for the period, the most effective being Two Little Red Shoes.

Nina Toye (?-?)

In the wake of the First World War, many who had survived the traumas of the conflict wanted nothing more than to forget its horrors in an orgy of self-indulgence.

One manifestation of this hedonistic urge was the craze for cocktails which swept Europe from America;

another was a renewed interest in all branches of escapist literature. Uniquely, the writer Nina Toye managed to cater for both appetites.

Her non-fiction work, *Drinks – Long & Short* (1925), written in collaboration with Arthur Adair, proved a popular handbook for any would-be barman or party host, while those interested in sensational literature could turn to her series of thrillers and historical romances.

One of Toye's most significant novels, *The Shadow of Fear* (1921), uses a supernatural storyline and in some ways foreshadows Daphne Du Maurier's masterpiece of Gothic romance, *Rebecca* (1938).

However, Du Maurier's subtle evocation of the oppressive and sinister atmosphere at Manderley can be sharply contrasted with Toye's more heavy-handed description of the haunted abbey's morbid aura which eventually drives the hero's wife insane.

Although not a great work, *The Shadow of Fear* is worthy of attention as an interesting twentieth century reinterpretation of traditional Gothic themes.

Selected bibliography

The Shadow of Fear by Nina Toye. London: William Heineman, 1921.
A modernised Gothic romance about the malevolent haunting of an ancient abbey. A rather dated work which is chiefly of interest to those researching the development of the Gothic novel.

Isabella Varley (1821-1897)

(Mrs George Linnaeus Banks)

Isabella Varley was born in Manchester at the height of the industrial revolution, but did not share the strong belief in modernisation held by many of her contemporaries. She preferred studying the past and her interests led her to amass a large collection of fossils and antiquarian material.

It was her marriage to the writer and poet George Linnaeus Banks that prompted Varley to attempt fiction. Her greatest success was a chronicle of northern industrial life, *The Manchester Man* (1876), which earned her a considerable reputation as a popular regional novelist and poet, despite the controversial realism of her work.

An ardent believer in the supernatural, she was an early collector of true ghost tales and legends and drew on them for her fiction. A published selection, *Through the Night* (1882), is very much a product of its time, permeated with the obsessions of middle class Victorian society.

However, because of their original subject matter and competent execution, many of the tales retain their interest and can still be read with considerable enjoyment.

Selected bibliography

Through the Night: Tales of Shades and Shadows by Mrs G. Linnæus Banks; Illustrated by G. C. Banks. Manchester: Abel Heywood & Son; London: Simpkin,

Marshall & Co., 1882.
A good, if slightly moralistic, collection of traditional ghost stories based on English legend and folklore.

Ellen Wood (1814-1887)
(Mrs Henry Wood)

Born in Worcester, Ellen Price married Henry Wood in 1836. She began her literary career by contributing items to popular magazines and this led to her becoming the proprietor and editor of the periodical, *Argosy*, in which much of her fiction would first appear.

Her greatest success came in 1861 with the publication of the novel, *East Lynne*, which has retained its popularity to this day. A prolific writer, Wood produced a large amount of fiction, including the *Johnny Ludlow* series of short stories. The tales, narrated by a teenage country boy, regularly feature mysterious and macabre incidents and were immensely popular throughout the Victorian period.

By the time of her death in 1887, Wood had sold over five million books.

Although often classed as a sensational novelist, Wood's literary talents are considerably more sophisticated than most contemporary writers of commercial fiction. She was perfectly capable of producing the over-sentimental and moralistic pulp fiction her public demanded, but could also create works of considerable literary merit, as *East Lynne* clearly demonstrates.

Several of Wood's ghost stories combine originality with great narrative skill and surely rank among the greatest of the Victorian era, comparable with those of Mrs Riddell and Mrs Gaskell. However, Wood has been largely neglected by anthologists in favour of the work of her contemporaries.

This lack of recognition may be due in part to the fact that her fiction was never collected in a single volume but remained scattered throughout numerous periodicals.

The common practice of magazines of the period to not attribute authorship may also mean that further ghostly tales by Wood remain undiscovered.

Selected bibliography

Featherston's Story: A Tale by Johnny Ludlow by Mrs Henry Wood. London: Richard Bentley and Son, 1889. *This novel-length tale includes numerous references to a ghostly figure and was a particular favourite of M.R. James. However, the supernatural content of the work is somewhat peripheral to the main plot.*

Adam Grainger and Other Stories by Mrs Henry Wood. New ed. London: Richard Bentley and Son, 1890.
Although the title novella is not supernatural, two of the accompanying short stories are of interest. Gina Montani *is an atypical Gothic tale set in Italy, while arguably the most successful tale is* A Mysterious Visitor. *The promising* All Souls' Eve *appears to be a conventional ghost story but is later rationalised when the 'ghost' turns out to be very much flesh and blood.*

The Shadow of Ashlydyat by Mrs Henry Wood. London: Richard Bentley, 1863.
This haunted house novel about a family curse is of above average quality for commercial fiction of the period.

Ghost Sightings

Introduction

Over the years, there have been many serious attempts to investigate supernatural phenomena and prove or disprove the existence of ghosts. Yet despite the subsequent debunking of much of this research, numerous accounts of ghostly events given in good faith still defy rational explanation.

This brief overview includes some of the most famous names associated with the exploration of ghostly phenomena, including dedicated researchers and investigators, as well as writers who faithfully preserved witness accounts of supernatural events. The strong association of the aristocracy with the true ghost story tradition is also evident here – somehow a stately home is not quite complete without its resident ghost.

Do ghosts exist? We simply don't know. But many would still argue, along with Eric Maple (see below), that 'purely on statistical grounds alone the case for their existence is securely established'.

DB

Catherine Crowe (1790-1876)

Crowe's tales, allegedly based on true events, would become an invaluable source of inspiration for many writers of ghostly fiction. She had a strong personal belief in spiritualism and it was her interest in the more morbid aspects of existence that friends blamed for her mental breakdown in the 1850s. Her books included, *Light and Darkness, or, The Mysteries of Life* (1850), a collection of stories written as 'faction'. The source material used by Crowe for her story, *The Lycanthropist*, was also used by Guy Endore as the basis for his famous novel, *The Werewolf of Paris* (1933).

Crowe's most popular book was *The Night Side of Nature, or, Ghosts and Ghost Seers* (1848), a non-fiction work recounting dreams, warnings, double-dreaming, doppelgängers, apparitions, haunted houses, and clairvoyance. It was highly influential in moulding the popular perception of ghostly phenomena for many years after its publication.

(See main entry on Catherine Crowe in this volume.)

Charles Lindley, Lord Halifax (1839-1934)

The 'true' ghost stories collected by Lord Halifax during his lifetime were published in 1936 as *Lord Halifax's Ghost Book*. In the foreword to the book (now available online), his son recalls how his father would recount some of the tales before bedtime:

Many is the time that after such an evening we children would hurry upstairs, feeling that the distance between the library and our nurseries, dimly lit by oil lamps and full of shadows, was a danger area where we would not willingly go alone, and where it was unsafe to dawdle.

He also quotes from the opening passage of a story his father wrote, which is included in the volume:

Where are the dead—those who have loved us and whom we have loved; and those to whom we may have done some irreparable injury? Are they gone from us forever, or do they return? Are they still amongst us, possessed of that undefined, mysterious, and awful existence which the ancient world attributed to the ghosts of the departed?... Between this world and that other which escapes our senses, we can neither explain the connecting link, nor admit an impassable barrier.

F.W.H. Myers (1843-1901)

Frederic William Henry Myers was a co-founder of the Society for Psychical Research. Together with Edmund Gurney and Frank Podmore, he wrote *Phantasms of the Living* (1886), one of the society's first substantial studies of the paranormal documenting various sightings of apparitions.

However, there were disagreements among the authors as Myers believed that apparitions were not hallucinations but real entities that existed in a dreamlike 'metetherial world', whereas his co-writers thought of them as telepathic hallucinations. Myers also promoted the concept of the 'subliminal self', a deep region of the unconscious that he claimed could account for supernatural events.

Myers had also collaborated with Gurney in 1884 to write an essay in which they recounted the story of a retired judge, Sir Edmund Hornby, who said he had been visited by a spirit. Myers and Gurney presented the tale as fact, but Hornby later admitted the account was false.

Gurney committed suicide in 1888 when he discovered that certain trusted mediums were frauds.

An overview of Myers' research into the unconscious mind was published posthumously in 1903 under the title, *Human Personality and Its Survival of Bodily Death*. His theories challenged the contemporary dominant orthodoxy of spiritualist beliefs.

When Myers died in Rome in 1901, many mediums claimed to have received communications from him.

Sir Arthur Conan Doyle (1859-1930)

In spite of his scientific training, Sir Arthur Conan Doyle was fascinated by the mysterious and supernatural and a number of his short stories deal with various aspects of the uncanny.

Following his wife's death in 1906 and that of a number of other family members during and just after the First World War, Doyle converted to the spiritualist cause and spent much of his later life investigating occult phenomena.

He was a member of The Ghost Club, founded in London in 1862 to investigate ghosts and hauntings. The club still exists today.

Doyle produced several non-fiction works on the subject, including his most significant spiritualist work, *The Edge of the Unknown* (1930).

Doyle also used photographs of the famous Cottingley

Fairies (now known to be a hoax) to illustrate an article he was writing, apparently believing they were genuine and evidence of supernatural phenomena. He was also convinced that his friend Harry Houdini possessed supernatural powers – a belief that led to their falling out.

After his death, a séance was held at London's Royal Albert Hall to enable Doyle to make an appearance from beyond the grave.

The chair set out for him on the stage remained empty, but many who attended the event said they felt his presence among them.

(*See main entry on Sir Arthur Conan Doyle in this volume.*)

Sir Ernest Nathaniel Bennett (1865-1947)

Sir Ernest Nathaniel Bennett, a politician, writer and explorer, was also a member of the Society for Psychical Research (founded in 1882 and still in existence today) and took a scientific approach to his extensive haunted house investigations.

His 1939 book, *Apparitions and Haunted Houses; A Survey of Evidence*, presents over 100 cases of supernatural phenomena reported to the society between the 1880s and 1930s, many recounted verbatim.

Bennett's stated aim was to 'awaken scientific curiosity' and to 'make some impression on two different classes of distinguished men – the scientists and the leaders of religion'.

Harry Price (1881-1948)

Harry Price, a British psychic researcher, both debunked and helped to strengthen belief in supernatural phenomena. He contributed to the exposure of various charlatan mediums as well as the 'spirit photographer' William Hope, but also believed that some mediums were genuine.

He is probably most famous for his investigation of Borley Rectory, in Essex, England, where he lived for a year between 1937 and 1938. There had been reports of supernatural phenomena at the rectory since it was built in 1862. Various sightings over the years included headless horsemen, the ghost of a nun, and an 'apparition' that appeared on several occasions. It came to be known as the 'most haunted house in Britain' following the publication in 1940 of Price's book about his experiences there *(The Most Haunted House in England: Ten Years' Investigation of Borley Rectory)*. The book was a sensation. In it, Price claims that on his first day there he saw a shadowy outline of a phantom nun.

The rectory was demolished in 1944 following extensive fire damage in 1939.

Shane Leslie (1885-1971)

Sir John Randolph Shane Leslie led a long and remarkable life, pursuing a wide and diverse range of interests. Although heir to a title, he was an early dropout, living for a period as a tramp and travelling widely throughout Europe.

During a trip through continental Europe, he met and befriended the celebrated Russian author Leo Tolstoy, who had rejected much of his own aristocratic heritage. Leslie later worked as a journalist, editor, lecturer and biographer as well as writing a number of fiction and non-fiction works.

Many of Leslie's books reflect his firm belief in the occult and much of his later life was spent investigating psychic phenomena at first hand, a pursuit made financially easier by his inheritance of the family fortune and title of Baronet in 1944.

Leslie's macabre fiction regularly made its first appearance in Cynthia Asquith's popular ghost story anthologies during the inter-war period. However, his lasting literary legacy probably lies in his non-fiction work, most notably, *Shane Leslie's Ghost Book* (1955). This work includes an introductory discussion of ghosts and supernatural phenomena, followed by a collection of 'true' accounts of ghostly experiences, including a spectral nun and priest as well as more unusual accounts such as the children who by 'listening' to an old altar table learned how to sing plainsong.

The Sitwells

The famous aristocratic Sitwell siblings, Edith, Osbert and Sacheverell, all pursued distinguished literary careers. In addition to his many works on music, art and architecture, Sacheverell (1897-1988) wrote *Poltergeists: An Introduction and Examination Followed by Chosen Instances* (1940) which includes an account of a young girl who despite being fast asleep would react to apparent poltergeist disturbances by breathing heavily and becoming flushed.

Sacheverell's older brother, Osbert (1892-1969), recounts in his autobiography, *Great Morning* (1947), a disturbing encounter with a palmist whom he visited with his fellow officers before the outbreak of World War One. He writes:

In each instance it appears, the cheiromant had just begun to read their fortunes, when, in sudden bewilderment, she had thrown the outstretched hand from her, crying, 'I don't understand it! It's the same thing again! After two or three months, the line of life stops short, and I can read nothing...'

The officers whose line of life could not be seen were to die in the war shortly after.

Eric Maple (1916-1994)

Eric Maple was a tireless researcher into folklore, witchcraft and the supernatural, perhaps influenced by his mother who in her younger days was a spiritualist medium.

His first publications were papers based on accounts given to him by people he interviewed in England who recounted their memories of alleged witches and their activities. Much of this material was also used in his later books, including *The Dark World of Witches* (1962) and *The Domain of Devils* (1966).

Arguably, his most famous work is *The Realm of Ghosts* (1964), in the preface of which he argues that:

The best authenticated phenomenon of history is the ghost. For thousands of years its activities have been observed and recorded by generation upon generation of competent witnesses, and purely on statistical grounds alone the case for its existence has been securely established.

The somewhat more lurid blurb on the back cover reads:

To those who find pleasure in pursuing the by-ways of terror this book will provide hours of disturbing reading. To the sceptic, who denies the supernatural, it offers a distracting venture into the world of ghouls, demons and dedicated ghost hunters.

The book is, in fact, a measured account of the author's rational research into the history of ghosts and their significance to humankind since ancient times.

Peter Underwood (b.1923)

Peter Underwood FRSA is an internationally renowned paranormal investigator and author of numerous books about ghosts (as a quick search on Amazon will testify).

Underwood spent many years investigating Borley Rectory, 'the most haunted house in England', tracing and interviewing almost every living person who had any dealings with it.

He also carried out extended investigations into the

'Greenwich ghost' photograph, described on Underwood's website as 'the best known genuine ghost photograph ever obtained'. Underwood is Harry Price's literary executor (see more on Harry Price above).

Diana Norman (1933-2011)

A British author and journalist best known for her historical and crime fiction, Norman also collaborated with members of the Historic Houses Association to write *The Stately Ghosts of England*, first published in 1963. The book is a collection of supernatural encounters and experiences reported by owners, guests and staff at various stately homes.

Norman was married to the British film critic, Barry Norman.

Bennison Books

Bennison Books has three imprints:

Contemporary Classics
Great writing from new authors

Non-Fiction
Interesting and useful works written by experts

People's Classics
Handpicked golden oldies by favourite and forgotten authors

Bennison Books is interested in publishing new
writing that's different, quirky, literary and original.
Authoritative works of reference will also be
considered for our non-fiction imprint.

Follow Bennison Books on <u>Twitter</u>
<u>twitter.com/BennisonBooks</u>
<u>Join Bennison Books on Facebook</u>
<u>facebook.com/BennisonBooks</u>
<u>Bennison Books</u>
<u>bennisonbooks.wordpress.com</u>

Bennison Books
A good book is a blessing

Made in United States
North Haven, CT
15 April 2023

35456364R00143